MW00616514

BRUTAL
SUBMISSION

EM BROWN

WIND COLOR PRESS

Copyright © 2023 by Em Brown

All rights reserved.

No portion of this book may be reproduced in any form without written permission from the publisher or author, except as permitted by U.S. copyright law.

CONTENTS

CHAPTER ONE

MARTINA ROSSI

B LOOD FROM MY BUSTED lip stains the rug I'm kneeling on, the intricate pattern of which starts to blur as my right eye swells shut from having connected with the fist of one of Vincent Xu's bodyguards. Two of them stand on either side of me, their guns drawn and aimed. My ribs hurt from where they kicked me, but I expect my pain to be short-lived.

A pair of Santonis, an expensive contrast to the men's loafers I'm wearing as part of my busboy uniform, steps into my view, and a deep voice says without sympathy, "You're dirtying my favorite Persian carpet with your blood."

I probably have minutes left to live. After trying to assassinate the head of the Black Dragon Triad, there's no way I make it out of this alive. The best I can hope for is a quick death. Like my mom's. And my dad's. And my baby brother's.

The only reason I managed to escape the bullets flying through our living room is because my older sister, Isabella, my idol, a second mother who showed me how to apply make-up, how to coordinate my clothes, how to make fun video clips on my phone, covered me with her own body. I remember her blood spraying over me, her body twitching against mine as we fell to the floor.

I was fifteen. More than five years later, I still have nightmares. The only thing keeping me from a full-blown case of PTSD is my determination to avenge the death of my family. I remember the faces of the men who had barged into our home with their assault rifles. One of them had a scar that ran down the right side of his face, from his eyebrow down to the middle of his cheek.

As I lay on the floor pretending to be dead that fateful day, I remember one of the killers, a bald guy with tattoos covering both arms, including the signature symbol of the Black Dragon Triad, asking the scarred man, "You sure Vincent wanted the wife and kids dead, too?"

"Vincent said to kill them all," replied scar face. "Besides, it's too late now."

"I didn't know there was gonna be kids here," the bald guy continued. "I've never heard the boss order the killing of a kid before."

At that, scar face turned his gun on his colleague and shot him dead. It took all of me not to flinch. Or maybe I did, just no one noticed. Lucky for me.

Or not. There were days it hurt so bad, when I thought I would suffocate from guilt, that I wish I had perished with my family. Why me? Why was it my beautiful sister who died in the ER? She was the angel in the family. She didn't deserve to die. My mother and five-year-old brother didn't deserve it, either. My father was perhaps less innocent, being the head of the Miami-based Rossi crime family. But that didn't make his death any more justified.

The man responsible for their deaths stands just over six feet tall and has to squat down to reach me. Vincent grabs my face, his long firm fingers digging into my cheeks, forcing me to look at him. In another life, I might have found him attractive. In his early thirties, he's in his prime with a strong jaw line, strikingly dark eyes, and lips that look like they can kiss as well as they can crush. Thanks to the work of the half-naked woman on the bed behind him, his button-up shirt is open, revealing a chiseled chest and six-pack.

While posing as a busboy named Ramon on Xu's private yacht, I've seen him turn the head of every woman aboard the yacht. There's more to him than a pretty face and cut body. He exudes a quiet confidence that's undeniable from a hundred feet away. But to me, he's a monster.

His eyes of ebony slice into me as if to cut out my secrets. When he speaks, it's with a calm that surprises me, given that I had come pretty damn close to killing him. Maybe there's been enough attempts on his life that he's no longer fazed by death. If he hadn't sensed my presence at the last second, my bullet would be lodged in the back of his head.

His thumb runs down my jawline, feeling the smoothness of my skin.

"You're just a boy," he appraises.

"Kill him already!" shrieks the woman from where she sits on his bed. She holds her bloody shoulder where the bullet intended for him had grazed. "Kill him!"

"Shut up or I'll kill you first," Vincent warns her.

She doesn't believe he's serious and hisses back, "You do that and you'll be missing out on all this."

She gives him a good look at her ample cleavage.

"You don't think I can get other pussy to fill your shoes?" Vincent returns placidly.

She draws in an indignant breath. "Don't you know who I am? I'm the daughter of—"

Before she can provide the name of her father, however, Vincent picks up my handgun from the floor and shoots her right between the eyes.

I nearly jump out of my skin. I don't know the woman, but she probably didn't deserve to die. If I could shoot as quickly and accurately as Vincent, I wouldn't be in my current predicament.

Still holding my face, Vincent turns back to me. "I've got to admit I'm impressed, kid."

I'm twenty-one years old, not a fucking kid. I stopped being a kid the day Vincent killed my family.

"You almost succeeded in killing me—came closer than anyone else," Vincent continues. "Speaks to your ingenuity. And the deficiencies of my security team."

One of his bodyguards clears his throat in discomfort.

If Vincent wasn't squeezing my face, I'd tell him to get this over with. Even though I didn't complete my mission, I didn't get to avenge my family, I'm ready to join them.

Mostly. My heartbeat is skittering all over the place. My base instinct wants to live, wants to survive.

"Who are you?" Vincent asks before glancing at the nameplate on my uniform. "I'm going to guess your real name isn't Ramon."

I stay silent, not wanting to give him the satisfaction of answering.

"Who hired you?" he tries instead before taking in the hate blazing from my eyes. "Ah, you weren't hired. This is personal."

He sounds intrigued and turns my head to view my profile. "But I don't know you."

When he turns me back, I look at my gun in his hand. Just shoot me already. I don't want to hear you talking things through the way the villains do at the end of a *Scream* movie.

As if reading my thoughts, Vincent says, "If you think you're going to get off easy by having your brains blown out, you don't know me well."

I try to contain the fear quaking my insides.

"There are so many more interesting ways to die," Vincent elucidates. "We could stab you with a dozen knives and let you bleed out over several days. Or we could torture you first, pour hot mercury into your eyes, slice off your kneecaps, pull out your teeth, and slowly starve you to death. Then there's old-fashioned options, like keelhauling, which would take advantage of the]=act that we're on a yacht in the middle of the sea. Since no one has ever gotten this close to killing me, I'll honor you by letting you choose."

None of those sound like good options. The only way I can get a quick death is if I force it.

"Which will it be?" he asks.

"Let go of my face and I'll tell you," I say, though the words come out half garbled.

As soon as he releases me, I lunge at him and my gun. Any second now, bullets will burn into my back, but Xu's bodyguards don't get a shot off because Vincent has grabbed me by the throat and slammed me to the ground beneath him. Instinctively, I try to pry off his chokehold, but his grip is too fierce. If he squeezes any harder, my eyes will pop out of their sockets. I claw at his hand and arm as I try to get my legs between us to kick him away, but he straddles me. I'm an average-sized woman, but atop me, he feels particularly large and heavy. He pauses in thought, undisturbed by the fact that I'm jamming my fingernails into his flesh and ripping off skin.

"Interesting," he says as he studies me closer. "If Ramon's not your real name, is it Ramona?"

My eyes widen. How did he guess I was female? Did he figure it out when he brushed up against my crotch? I continue to struggle against his grip. Right now I don't care if he figures out who I really am, but I have one secret I can't let him discover, a secret I plan to take to my grave.

Everyone else in my family are betas, or neutrals, but my parents must have been carriers of the recessive omega gene because I'm one hundred percent omega. I take illicit, super expensive drugs to suppress my submissive omega traits. I can't say why, but I have a strong sense that Vincent Xu is an alpha, the top of the hierarchy. I would rather kill myself than submit to him.

Realizing I can't loosen his powerful grip around my throat, I go for his eyes. He jerks his head away. Next, I feel a sharp, exact pressure on my neck before blacking out.

CHAPTER TWO

VINCENT XU

T HE WOMAN PASSED OUT on my bedroom floor doesn't look familiar, and I never forget a face.

"Tie her up in the dungeon," I instruct two of my men as I study the 9mm I hold. It's a nice piece with high-performance sighting ability. The US Navy Seals use a version of this full-size pistol. This woman meant business.

I hand the gun over to Esen, the head of my security team and my cousin once removed. His father is Mongolian and whom Esen inherited his stout physique from. Esen also likes to pump weights, which adds to his largess. If he bulks up any more, he'll be physically useless to me. He's lucky I keep him around for his brains and not his brawn.

While additional men remove the body of the woman in my bed, I look in the mirror to assess the slash marks across my cheek. My would-be assassin was going for my eyes. I should gouge hers out as payback for the attempt. It would be a shame because she has very pretty eyes, at least from what I can tell of her good one. A vibrant hazel color with flecks of gold. If I had a nice bone in my body, I would let her have some ice to help reduce the swelling in her other eye and some aspirin to take away the pain.

But what's the sense in being nice? I was nice once. Fate screwed me over anyway. Hit me where it hurt the most. Took away an innocent life—one I valued more than my own—and left me to live in pain. So I'm paying that forward.

"You want me to get the doc for you, boss?" asks Esen.

"For this?" I reply dismissively as I glance at the claw marks on my left hand and arm. My assassin is a feisty one, a fighter. I'm glad. It'll make it more interesting when I break her.

"I'll shower off the blood," I tell Esen. "When I'm done, I want a report on how this kid made it into my room with a fucking Sig Sauer."

"Yes, boss."

The lacerations sting beneath the shower as I rinse myself off, but my body has seen far worse. A concussion. Broken arm. Bullets in my ribs and legs. The worst was a spinal cord injury I took from falling out of the fourth floor of a building. Even for an alpha, it took a lot of fucking qigong work to heal.

As the hot water streams over my head and face, I think back to "Ramon," trying to place her. I can't, though I'm good with faces. I thought she was a teenage boy at first, but she might be in her early twenties. No older than that, though. How can I not recognize someone who wants to kill me this badly?

After my shower, I slide into a robe and sit outside on the balcony to watch the moon rise over the Caribbean Sea. Esen joins me outside after dismissing the maids who are putting new sheets on my bed.

"My guys are interviewing everyone, but we've got nothing so far, boss," he informs me. "Ramon Sanchez was cleared, and the photo ID in the employee database is hers."

"Does a Ramon Sanchez really exist?"

"Don't know."

I pour myself a shot of *baijiu*. "Either way, I think she has someone on the inside."

"We'll dig them out, boss."

For a second, I wonder if I should have let this woman succeed in killing me. If it weren't for personal unfinished business, there's nothing left for me to live for. I don't have close family, and I don't get enough satisfaction heading the Black Dragon Triad anymore. After working my way to the top and wresting power from the former heir apparent, I built Black Dragon into one of the most feared and successful criminal organizations spanning both sides of the Pacific. I haven't implemented succession plans, but there's no shortage of people wanting to take my place. The organization will survive me.

"You look through her cabin? Her possessions?" I ask.

"Yes. Nothing of interest except some drugs. Ours. But just a small amount."

I recognize the capsules in the small plastic bag he holds. They're omega blockers, a product manufactured and sold by the Black Dragon Triad.

"Ramon" just keeps getting more and more interesting. Not only is he a woman, he's an omega.

How unlucky for her.

CHAPTER THREE

VINCENT

AFTER I'VE CHANGED INTO a casual dress shirt and slacks, I make my way to "the dungeon" with my drink in hand. I keep wondering who this "Ramon" is. Very little catches me by surprise. It's as if this woman came out of nowhere. What in the world did I do to her to make her want to kill me? I still haven't ruled out that she's a possible hitman, but there's no denying the hatred I saw in her eyes. Now I'm fucking curious.

I can't remember the last time I was curious about anything. At least, not in the past three years. Except for my goal of settling a blood debt, I've lost interest in most things. I took the Black Dragon Triad, a successful international criminal organization, to new heights, and while there are opportunities to do even more, I don't have that ambition.

I do, however, want to know more about this "Ramon Sanchez," then rip her a new one for trying to kill me. Her biggest mistake was not succeeding because I will have her begging for death when I'm done. Since becoming head dragon, there have only been two attempts on my life, and they were early on. Once word got out that I'm meticulous and ruthless when it comes to payback, no one has dared attempt to take me down.

So who does this little omega think she is?

My first thought was that she's a jilted lover, but I haven't had a relationship in the past three years. Not since...

I've slept with women, but I never give the impression that they are anything more than a fuck.

"Vincent, you dog," says Charlie Wong as he drapes an arm around me, "I saw you walking off with Camellia Ma. That is one hot piece of pussy."

At thirty-five years of age, Charlie has been a part of the Black Dragon for two decades. He's passionate and loyal, the scar slicing through his right eye a reminder of how much he risks for the triad. If and when I retire, I'd consider handing the reins over to someone like Charlie.

The other person I'm considering is Yang Mi. She's smarter than Charlie but hasn't been in the business as long.

"So how was it?" Charlie asks. "How was her pussy? Ten out of ten, you'd do her again?"

That's one of Charlie's favorite phrases when it comes to women.

"I wouldn't know. I shot her instead," I reply.

"Oh. Shit. Just as well. I heard she's a spoiled bitch."

"She's been irritating this whole trip."

Camellia is the daughter of the head of the Ma Family Triad. They pissed me off when they tried to infringe on my drug business, going so far as to take down one of my labs where a good chunk of my omega blockers are made. I had intended to ransom Camellia, but her death works too.

"Ma will want revenge," Charlie notes of Camellia's father. "You want me to take preventative action?"

"Let's talk it over later. I have to tend to something first," I say.

The dungeon is essentially a windowless basement just above the water line of the yacht. It houses a plethora of BDSM furniture: vertical cages, horizontal cages, St. Andrew's cross, a rack, a wooden pony, a barrel, and the pillory. Along the wall are cases filled with BDSM paraphernalia: floggers, whips, canes, paddles, chains, herds, gags, and electrical equipment, some running into thousands of dollars.

"Ramon" is shackled between two posts, her arms pulled to the top corners of the posts and her ankles stretched shoulder-width apart. She hasn't regained consciousness yet, and her head hangs down toward her chest.

To wake her up, I throw my drink in her face. She gasps, possibly at the sting of the alcohol upon her cut lip.

"Give me your real name and I'll go easier on you," I tell her.

She looks at me skeptically with her one good eye. "Easier in what way?"

"Like maybe I'll kill you after three days instead of letting you suffer for an entire week."

She doesn't say anything, but her glare tells me to go fuck myself.

"Coming from me, it's a generous offer," I say.

She seems to take that into account. "Ramon Sanchez."

For a second, I consider slapping her. Hard. And telling the bitch that it's not wise to lie to me. Instead, I set my drink glass down on a nearby table before standing within inches in front of her.

I grab her jaw. She flinches in pain.

"Funny, you don't look like a Ramon Sanchez," I say.

I look her features over carefully. Nothing Latin stands out. She looks more Mediterranean. If it weren't for her bruised and swollen eye, she'd probably look attractive. Her lips, though cracked and bleeding, are sensuous.

"That the name you're sticking with?" I ask.

Though there's fear in her eyes—she wouldn't be an intelligent human being if she wasn't about to piss her pants right now—she holds my gaze. "Yes."

I have better things to do than to play games with her, but if she insists on them, she's going to learn that there's a price to pay.

Releasing her jaw, I drop my hand to the top button of her white collared shirt, part of the uniform worn by the servers and kitchen staff.

I undo the button. "Ramon, eh?"

She frowns as I undo all the buttons and gasps when I yank the shirt open to reveal the linen she uses to bind her breasts flat.

"Ramona," she corrects.

I get a pair scissors and tap the blades gently above her sternum. "You sure about that?"

She nods. "I meant to say Ramona to begin with."

"Let's be sure."

"It's Ramona!" she insists as I begin to cut away her bindings.

She wriggles a little at first but then realizes too much movement might make the scissors cut awry. Her breasts burst through the bindings. They're a nice handful, perky, natural, and not overly large. I cup an orb, assessing it as if I'm cradling a mango to determine its ripeness. I look into her eyes, satisfied that she hates me even more now.

"So it does appear Ramona is more fitting than Ramon," I say, "but let's be extra sure."

Her eyes flare wide. I start to cut the way at her slacks. This time she strains against her bonds without caring that she might get nicked by the scissors.

Seeing her fury, I bet she wants to call me every name in the book, but she also knows that won't change things. There's nothing she can do. I can have my way with her, do anything I want with her.

And I'm going to.

After slicing through the crotch of her pants to reveal her plain cotton briefs, I jam my hand between her legs. She tries her best to evade my touch, grunting when I grab her pussy through her underwear.

"Now that we've established that Ramona is a more appropriate name than Ramon, let's try for your real name."

"That is my real name," she says and adds beneath her breath, "*stronzo*."

As I suspected, she isn't Latina. She's Italian. And American. And though I was born in New York and spent most of my life in this country, I'm not monolingual. I speak fluent English, Cantonese, Mandarin, and Russian. And I have a working knowledge of Italian, having done some collaborations with the mafia.

This little omega thought she could slip in *stronzo* without me noticing? That isn't very respectful, and she's going to pay dearly for that.

Chapter Four

" ...STRONZO."

Even though I hear her clearly, I grab her cheeks, pressing them harshly into her teeth, and ask, "What was that last part?"

She says nothing and only looks at me as if she believes her stare can kill people.

I pull her face closer to me. "I asked you a question."

When she still doesn't answer, I grasp one of her nipples and pinch it cruelly. "We could do this all night long, or you can answer me."

"*Stronzo*," she squeals.

I'm still bruising her cheeks, so she isn't able to articulate well, but I know what she said. Even so, I pretend like I didn't. "What was that?"

"*Stronzo*," she pants as her body tenses further with my continued torture of her nipple. "I said *stronzo*."

I release her nipple and her face and give her left cheek a pat. "Now why would you call me that?"

She glares at me. "If you need me to spell it out, you're not only an asshole, you're *stupido*."

I raise an amused brow. She's a bit of a hothead. And not as smart as I thought.

"I admire your spirit," I say. "Your intelligence, however, is wanting. But that doesn't bother me. The more you dish it, the more reason I have to punish you."

To demonstrate my point, I pinch her other nipple and give it a brutal twist. She does her best to contain her cries.

"I like being called a *stronzo*," I inform her. "I promise you I'll live up to that name. In fact, you can call me Master Stronzo. Do it. Call me Master Stronzo."

In a bit of a quandary, she doesn't respond right away as she tries to figure out if it's better to do as I say or not.

"When I tell you to do something, you do it," I explain as I thrust my hand into her underwear, "because if you don't do it, and promptly, I'm

going to have to discipline you for your disobe-
dience."

Threading my fingers through her pubic hair,
I start to pull. Against her will, her body bows
toward me.

She whimpers, then relents. "Master Stronzo."

Slowly, I let go of her bush. "Now what am I
going to call you?"

It's a rhetorical question, but before proceed-
ing, I pause because I can catch the faintest
scent of her pussy. I wonder, if she weren't taking the omega blockers, how would she respond
to my pheromones? I let my hand linger in her
panties.

"Pet," I finally continue. "*Animale domestico.*
Because that's what you'll be for the next week
or so until you die: my pet. You'll obey my commands, sleep where I let you sleep, eat what I let
you eat, and take your punishments like a good
little bitch."

"You said I could die in three days."

She sounds like a kid protesting that they had
been promised several cookies, not just one.

"That was only if you told me your real name,"
I inform her.

"I told you my name."

I pat her cheek. "Okay. Have it your way."

Going over to a dresser, I select a pair of alligator clamps and several small weights to hang off them. She looks at them, perplexed.

"New to nipple play?" I ask before I pull at one nipple and attach the clamp to the base of the bud.

Her mouth drops as she sucks in her breath, looking surprised at how much a small little thing can hurt. I attach the second clamp. Her gasp quivers.

I give her a smile. "We're just getting started...Ramona."

Now there is a chance Ramona Sanchez is her real name, but I'm not betting on it. I hang a weight onto the nipple clamp and watch as her eyes widen, one much more than the other. At first, her breath comes quick and shallow, then she tries to breathe through the pain with longer breaths. When her gaze meets mine, it's to tell me she thinks I'm some kind of sicko.

"Just like you called me," I tell her, "*stronzo.*"

I hang a weight on the other clamp and tap the weight to make it swing. She grimaces.

"Got two more," I say, holding up more weights.

She eyes them with dread and braces herself before I add them, making her grunt and tense.

"Still sticking with Ramona Sanchez?" I ask, but her focus is elsewhere—on her nipples, no doubt. To get her attention, I slap her. "I asked you a question, pet."

"Yes," she answers through gritted teeth.

It shouldn't matter to me if she wants to take her name to her grave, but I want to know because I've never seen hate as intense as what blazes from her eyes. Who is she? Is she working for someone? And who's helping her?

I unclip one of the clamps and move it to the tip of her nipple, where it hurts more.

"Oh, shit..." she whimpers as her legs tremble.

I do the same with the other clamp.

"Having fun yet, Ramona?" I ask wickedly.

After watching her struggle to adjust to the pain, I return to the chest of drawers for more weights.

I hold them up for her to see. "How many of these do you think we can attach before they tear off your cute little nipples?"

"Please," she whispers.

"Please what? Please add more weights to my nipples?"

"Please...I'll tell you my name."

I wait while she takes in a deep breath and lifts her head to meet my gaze.

"Irene," she says. "Lazzarini."

The blood drains from my face. For several seconds, the world stops. When I recover, I cross over to her, grab her by the throat, and start squeezing the life out of her.

CHAPTER FIVE

MARTINA

MY BODY STARTS THRASHING, which makes the weights pull even more at my nipples, but that's a secondary concern to the air being choked out of me. The shackles about my wrists and ankles don't give. There's no way I can stop Vincent from strangling me to death. I should welcome this early death. It's better than being tortured for days first.

But I hate suffocation. It's the manner of death I fear the most.

When I was a young kid, I got trapped underneath an inflatable boat I had taken with my older cousins out on a pond at night. I wasn't a strong swimmer, and in the dark waters, I couldn't tell which way was up. In my panic, I sucked in water. It was terrifying.

My sister was the one who saved me. I remember her scolding my cousins for not having put a life vest on me. They explained they thought I could swim.

I never did learn because I was too scared of the water.

So even though I had thought I was ready to die, I fight for my life, doing everything I can to wrest myself from the vise of Vincent's grip.

"Bullshit!" he accuses, shaking me.

I feel myself starting to black out, but his chokehold relaxes just enough for me to take in a little bit of air. He still looks furious, though.

"No fucking way your name is Irene," he spits in my face.

It wasn't the name I had intended to say if I had time to think. It's just what popped into my head. I don't even know any Irenes. Maybe one of my grandmother's friends was named Irene.

"I was named after my grandmother," I squeak, mystified that he's so hung up on a name.

He snorts. "Irene isn't very Italian. Not like- Lazzarini."

"My maternal grandmother was Greek," I say. That part is true.

Abruptly, he releases me. I frantically take in the air I had been deprived of. Holy shit. What the hell?

Vincent runs his hand through his hair and paces before me. His thoughts are elsewhere. When he glances at me, I can see the vein at his temple throb. I'm scared he's going to grab the clamps and rip my nipples off.

Instead, he abruptly leaves, closing the door behind him. I'm alone. This is a good thing. I think. Except the clamps and weights are still hanging off my nipples. I've never hated having nipples more than I do now. What's the purpose of them being so sensitive? I would give anything not to have nipples right now. The pain the poor buds are enduring far exceed the bruising of my ribs and eye. I wish I could pass out.

I try to consider my options. Is there any way out of this? Can I negotiate with Vincent? Would I want to? But it's hard to think straight when it feels like I'd rather be breast-feeding a pair of baby alligators.

Several minutes pass like hours before the door opens. Shit. What's he going to do to me now? But it's not Vincent. It's two of his thugs, possibly coming to beat me up some more.

To my surprise and relief, they remove the nipple clamps. I almost thank them. They also unshackle my wrists, but not to free me. They pinion my arms behind me and cuff my wrists together. Even though it's two to one, I do my best to resist their efforts on the small chance that I can break free. I'm naturally athletic, and I spent two years training daily with a martial artist. I manage to kick the taller of the two in the balls when they make the mistake of un-shackling both my ankles at the same time. He curses while the other guy slams me face down to the ground. He straddles me and pins my ankles down so his buddy can bind them with rope. After they're done hog-tying me, the taller one turns me onto my side and kicks me in the stomach for payback. I curl into a fetal position, trying to protect my organs from his next kick.

"Boss didn't say we could do anything other than tie her up," the shorter guy says. "Remem-ber when Johnny freelanced and accidentally got that informant killed? Boss messed Johnny up big time."

"Yeah, yeah," the taller guy says nervously. "I didn't kick this bitch too hard."

"Good. The boss obviously has plans for her."

"What if she tells boss what I did?"

"Boss probably already knows. There are cam-eras down here."

"Fuck me."

I glance with them toward one video camera at the corner of the ceiling. There's another pointed at the door and a third one aimed at the center of the room where I was strung up.

The thugs leave me curled up on the floor. I struggle against my bonds, but they're secure around my wrists and ankles. Even though my body hurts in many different places, I gather my thoughts. I'm not dead yet, so maybe I still have a shot at accomplishing my goal of killing Vincent Xu. But first, I need to take my omega blocker. It won't help if I'm distracted. I have a capsule in my back pocket, but it's not easy to get to since my pants are torn and hanging around my hips. Eventually, I wriggle the capsule out. Now the challenge is getting it into my mouth. I can place the capsule on the floor and swallow it from there.

I drop the capsule, then roll and rotate my body to get to it. But before I can get my mouth to the capsule, the door opens. In walks Vincent. His two thugs follow him.

I rush toward the capsule, but Vincent plants his shoe against my shoulder, stopping me.

He picks up the capsule. "What's this?"

Taking his foot off me, he squats down so he can better look in my eyes. "This something important to you, pet?"

He's not going to let me take it, but I need my daily dosage.

"You want to tell me what this is?"

"Steroids," I lie.

He must see the worry in my face because he gives me an evil grin. "I think this is something much more special than steroids."

To my dismay, he opens the capsule, spilling the powdery contents onto the floor. Shit. What should I do now? I can't go without the omega blocker. Worried that he might try to stop me, I quickly lick as much of the medication off the floor as I can. It tastes rancid, and my dry mouth could really use some water to wash it down with.

Vincent lets me clean the floor of the substance before pointing to some that had landed on his designer Italian shoes, saying, "You missed a spot."

CHAPTER SIX

VINCENT

As I wait to see what she will do, I keep thinking to myself that there's no way her name is Irene. It's just not a common name in this day and age, and it so happens to be the one name I never wanted to hear again. There's only one Irene in my life.

After hearing it for the first time in three years, it hits me like a wrecking ball. I actually had to go back up to my room and gather myself.

It's just a name. A name that meant the world to me at one point. But that was years ago. It should mean nothing to me now. Except I have unfinished business. And until I avenge her death, I can't even face her memorial tablet.

As for this Irene, she won't be long in this world. By the consternation on her face, I'm guessing that she would rather jab a pencil in her eye than lick my shoe. But she must have wanted her omega blocker bad because, after swallowing her grimace with as much relish as someone would swallow their own puke, she sticks out her tongue and licks the white powdery substance off my loafers.

I could have tossed away her omega blocker if I was certain that would make her more miserable. I imagine torturing her until she begs for death. I had considered leaving the clamps and weights on her nipples. Eventually her nipples would rot from loss of blood circulation. But I have other plans for her nipples.

And letting her have her omega blockers isn't out of line with my objective. Without the blockers, her body would ultimately become receptive to my touch. Her body would surrender, possibly before the battle had even begun. With the blockers, she'll fight me instead. But resisting will render the battle bloodier when I finally invade her body and demolish her.

Plus, it's damn entertaining to watch her clean my floor and shoe.

"That's a good pet," I say.

She doesn't say anything, but I can tell my words burn her ears.

"You should thank me for letting you have your omega blocker," I tell her.

She stares silently into nothing.

"Let's hear it, pet."

She doesn't comply.

Squatting down, I fist my hand in her hair and yank her head back so that her gaze meets mine. I have the feeling she'd spit in my face if she could muster enough saliva.

"Last chance," I say in a low tone.

It doesn't matter to me if she obeys or not, she's going to suffer regardless. But her hatred of me must run deep if she won't give in on such a small matter as thanking me. She has to know she's better off placating me. Or maybe, because she knows she's going to die, she at least wants to do it on her own terms. I'm intrigued.

"There's a fine line between stubbornness and stupidity," I tell her.

Roughly, I release her and stand up. I instruct my men to hang her from the ceiling. They undo the bonds around her wrists and retie them in front of her. There's a hook I use for suspension bondage, and they hang her off that like she's a slab of meat in a butcher's shop. Her feet dangle several inches off the floor. Her slacks have slipped off her hips and pool around her feet.

I stand in front of her. "So far you've accumulated two punishments. One for being insolent earlier. Two for not saying thank you. It's too bad your mother didn't teach you how to be more polite."

Anger flares in her one good eye. So the subject of her mother is a touchy one.

I gaze at her nipples, still hard from the clamp and weight treatment. I brush my knuckle over one of them. She gasps.

"Seems like they're ripe for more attention," I note. "Don't you agree?"

She stares ahead into space, as if I don't exist. This bitch doesn't want to give me anything.

That's fine. The higher she sits on her high horse, the more painful her fall.

Grasping her jaw harshly, I nod her head up and down. "The answer is yes."

I turn her gaze toward one of the cameras. "You and I are going to put on a show, pet, to demonstrate what happens when you insist on being a willful brat. That video camera is going to record everything. And when we're done, who should we send the recording to? Mom and Dad? A husband or boyfriend?"

She doesn't flinch at any of those options.

"Wife or girlfriend?" I add.

Nothing. Her response surprises me. I can already tell she's not the best at hiding her feelings. The thought of having a loved one witness her assault should've made her skin crawl. So maybe she doesn't have family. Or maybe she's a sociopath.

"Scissors," I direct to Jack, the shorter but more skilled of my henchmen.

He brings me a pair, which I use to cut away her shirt after releasing her jaw. I hand the scissors back to Jack, then reach down to yank off her pants and shoes.

She puts on a stoic front, as if it doesn't bother her that she's practically naked in front of her enemy. Her lashes, however, flutter when I grab the front of her panties and twist them, making the fabric dig into her flesh before ripping the garment from her.

Grabbing her chin, I pry her mouth open and stuff in her underwear. Resisting, she tries to spit it out, but I shove it deeper.

"Gag her," I instruct Vlad, a tall blend of Russian, Korean, and Chinese.

Vlad has a sadistic streak and more than willingly straps a red ball gag over her mouth to keep the underwear in place.

"Good thing you didn't wear boxers," I remark to her. "That would've been harder to stuff in your mouth, though it would've been interesting to try."

I step back to admire her naked form, caressing her curves with my gaze. If it were possible to hate even more, she's there.

I go over to the dresser and bring back a basket of twine and clothespins, which I set down on a nearby chair. After unwinding some twine, I clip it to her arm, near her armpit, with a clothespin. I apply another a few inches from the first, working my way up her arm. I cut the string and start to do the same with her other arm.

"I think my men like what they see," I say as I start to make a third zipper along the left side of her body, pinching her breast, rib, waist, hip, and thigh with the clothespins.

"Maybe I should let them have their way with you," I muse aloud as I make a clothespin zipper down the right side of her body. "Would you like that?"

She stares straight ahead. At this point, she probably expects to be raped, but I don't see much fear in her eyes. She has mental toughness to her. It's going to take more than the average vanilla rape to break her.

Good thing I excel in non-vanilla.

CHAPTER SEVEN

MARTINA

"SPREAD HER LEGS," VINCENT instructs his two minions.

With rope, his men tie my ankles to separate iron rings on the floor spaced more than shoulder width apart. Vincent holds up another clothespin.

I can handle the clothespins. No big deal. They're not worse than the kick in the stomach I received from the taller goon. I can also handle being naked before these guys. I don't give a fuck. Well, maybe a little. At first. But I'm not ashamed of my body, and I sure as hell don't want to give them the satisfaction of feeling degraded.

I don't flinch when Vincent applies clothespins to random places like my eyebrow and my earlobe. It's hard not to react when he clips them to my nipples, though, because my nipples are still extra sensitive from their prior treatment. But I do my best to just stare ahead silently while he attaches clothespins to my labia and clit.

Even if they rape me, I'm not going to fold for Vincent in the way that he wants. I'd sooner slit my throat, which I would if I could find something sharp. The scissors he used earlier are a possibility.

As if reading my thoughts, Vincent says, "You know there are fates worse than death."

And I hope you suffer just such a fate.

"I could sell you off to a human trafficker," he expands. "How would you like to get raped every day for the rest of your life? Or until you're too used up to attract anyone anymore?"

I can't resist looking at him to silently say, "You sick motherfucker. There's got to be a special place in hell for assholes like you."

He returns my gaze. "I just made you hate me more, didn't I? Well, we're just getting started, pet. You don't seem that intimidated by a sex trafficker, so how about I sell you to a breeder?"

My resolve quivers at that. Rape is one thing. Being impregnated then having to bear the child of one's rapist is a whole other level. And my heart would break having to birth a child into slavery.

"You have several childbearing years left in you," he continues. "These hips look like they can bear a good number of pups."

I feel sick when he grabs my hips. I'd rather have more clothespins on me than his hands.

"A pretty little omega like you is worth at least half a million," he says. "Maybe I can get twice that if you're a virgin. There's always some rich, sick fuck who will pay good money to do a virgin. You a virgin, pet?"

Thank God I'm not. Vincent Xu is the last person on earth I would want to give my virginity to.

"No comment? No worries. I can find out for myself."

He presses the tip of his finger at my opening. How I wish my vagina was a guillotine that could lop off his finger! His digit presses into me. I'm actually surprised he doesn't just shove himself into me. Instead, he works his finger in slowly, almost like that of a lover. Maybe he thinks this is worse for me.

"You're tight," he notes. "Maybe you're a virgin. Or maybe you haven't done it in a while."

Because I've been too busy tracking you down and finding a way to kill you, you stronzo. Damn. That insult doesn't have the same impact now that he's claimed it for his name.

His finger continues to burrow into me. "You usually this dry?"

Without lubrication, his finger grates against my tender flesh.

He pushes in deeper. Damn, he has long fingers.

"Maybe taking those omega blockers isn't to your benefit. If you had slick, this wouldn't be as uncomfortable."

He has a point. But I don't want any of this, and I certainly don't want him thinking I could desire him in any way. Without the omega blockers, my body would submit to him. I wouldn't stand a chance. And I need to stay focused, to be alert for any opportunity that might arise.

His finger is deep inside me.

"No hymen," he says. "Doesn't mean you're not a virgin, but without a hymen, it'll be harder to sell you as one."

He doesn't sound devastated, but I don't expect him to. As the head of a hugely successful criminal organization, he doesn't care if he misses out on half a million dollars.

"That's okay. It would've been fun to pop your cherry, but I have other ways of making it hurt as badly as if you were losing your virginity for the very first time. "

God, I want to kill this man so badly.

He takes a step back, and I'm glad for the space, glad that he's no longer breathing on me, glad not to feel the warmth emanating from his body.

His fingers wrap around the extra string at the end of the clothespin line on my left arm. Our gazes meet for a silent beat before he yanks the clothespins off my arm. I cry out, my body shaking. I actually prefer having the clothespins on me than experiencing them coming off. He drinks in my reaction before toying with the clothespin attached to my clit. I brace myself when he reaches for the end of the string pinned to the right side of my body.

"Fuck!" I scream into my panties and the gag.

He waits until my body stops quivering before asking, "Did that hurt, pet?"

My skin still tingles. It feels like I've been bitten and slapped where the clothespins were. But I can take this. Only two more of these clothespin zippers. I watch him reach for the string dangling from my right arm. I brace my-self.

He sees this and says to one of his men, "Hood her."

The one with Eurasian features grabs what looks like a small black pillowcase, which he fits over my head. Now I can't see anything.

"Which one to unzip next?" I hear Vincent muse aloud.

Whichever. Just get this the fuck over with.

But I wait. And wait. The air in the hood becomes warm. I want more oxygen. My mouth is so parched.

The instant I relax my body a little, the clothespins come flying off my arm. I hear them scattering to the floor.

My arms are sore from bearing the weight of my body, which wants to crumple to the floor. But there's one clothespin zipper left.

I've got this.

But I don't.

Because someone—probably Vincent—pinches my nose shut through the hood. With my mouth stuffed to the brim with my panties and the ball gag, I can't breathe. I flail against my bonds.

I don't want to die this way!

But I start to feel lightheaded and weak. My chest is heavy.

Please let me breathe. Please—

He releases my nose. Just as I desperately fill my lungs with air, the clothespins are yanked from my body. I choke on my own scream. My body is confused, torn between relief and pain. Should it thrash or relax?

God, get me out of this...

Chapter Eight

Because I am a sadistic fuck, her thrashing about turns me on. She has a nice body. Curves in all the right places but toned and strong. I like that she has a supple ass, and her tits are natural, not overblown for her size and shape. But most of all, I like how reactive she is, despite her best efforts to be stoic. I continue to pinch her nose shut until her struggles diminish. When I release her, I hear her wheezing beneath the hood as she sucks in oxygen.

Getting more clothespins, I say, "Let's put some more of these bad boys on you."

I apply the clothespins to the most sensitive parts of her body and adjust the placements of the ones already on her in case she's turning numb beneath them. Above her, a beam runs across the ceiling.

"Retie her ankles to that," I instruct Jack and Vlad.

She kicks against them, though her resistance is futile. She's better off saving her strength.

After they're done, it looks like she's doing the splits in midair. With her legs spread wide, her pussy is completely exposed.

I take the clothespin off her clit and caress the wrinkled bud with my thumb. She tries to jerk away from my touch. Even with the omega blockers, her body responds against her will. I feel her clit swell ever so slightly. I manage to attach three of the clothespins to the small pink nub. I apply several more to her labia and all along her inner thighs. Stepping away, I select a leather flogger with long thin tails. Normally, for a beginner, I would go for a flogger made from a softer hide and that delivers less sting.

But I want this to hurt.

Flogger in hand, I circle her and assess the potential targets. She has smooth supple skin, perfect for marking up. Unfurling the tails, I lash it against a buttock. She jumps at the impact.

"That's me being nice, pet," I tell her. "I could've started with a more sensitive part of your body, like this one..."

I backhand the flogger against the side of her breast and watch it wobble.

I walk to the front of her and whack her other breast. My strikes are precise from years of practice. For the inside of her thigh, I land just the tips for a more stinging effect. I slap her other inner thigh for symmetry. With the hood over her head, she can't tell where the flogger will land, so she tenses her whole body. I flog almost every available inch of her body: her legs, her breasts, her arms. I avoid her internal organs for now. I don't want to injure her and have her die on me before it's time.

I brush my fingers over the clothespins attached to her pussy and her clit before taking a step back and whacking her between the legs, sending a few clothespins flying. I hear a muffled shriek from beneath the hood. I wonder which is worse: getting her pussy flogged or getting whipped where I'm about to next.

I flick the tails against the bottom of her bare foot. She cries out against her gag.

"Did you know there were so many sensitive nerve endings in your foot?" I ask as I gently run my thumb where the flogger had struck. I flog her there again. She grunts and strains.

"There are a lot of delicate bones in the foot," I explain. "Bastinado was a serious form of punishment in many cultures."

I strike her foot harder. She screams louder. I again caress the bottom of her foot with my thumb before kissing it with the leather tails. Her body jerks forcefully against her bonds.

"Next time we'll try using a ruler to see which implement you like better for your bastinado."

I go back to flogging the other parts of her body till she's blushing all over. I strike the clothespins off her nipples, then come at her pussy from different angles. But her cries are definitely loudest when I flog the bottoms of her feet.

Changing my grip, I hold the other end of the handle, which bears the shape of a dildo. I run the bulge of the handle along her pussy.

"Normally I would have my subs thank me for their flogging for their punishments," I say, "but I'll let it go this time since you can't really talk."

I press the end of the handle into her enough so that she can appreciate the good-sized girth.

With my mouth near her ear, I ask into the hood, "Want to guess how long the handle of this flogger is? Given how tight your pussy is,

I'm betting this is thicker and longer than anything else you've had in your cunt."

I pull the hood off her so I can see her reaction. "You ever had a foreign object shoved into you? A beer bottle? A baseball bat? How about a shower brush? That'll scrape your insides. We could throw some chili onto the bristles so it stings extra bad."

She doesn't even blink. As if she's heard all of this before. Or maybe she's too drained to process what I'm saying.

As I consider what to do with her next, my assistant, Ming, enters. Ming has been in the business for over forty years and served the dragon before me. At first, I wasn't sure I could trust Ming, but he doesn't have ambitions for himself. He just likes being a loyal supporter as long as he and his family are treated well.

"You have a call from Jose," Ming tells me, holding a phone.

He glances over at "Ramona." I'm not referring to her by that other name, even if it's her real name.

"Want me tell him you'll call him back?" Ming asks.

"It doesn't matter what she overhears," I answer. "She's not going anywhere. And she's not going to live long enough to tell anyone about it."

Ming hands me the phone.

"We intercepted a truck hauling a shipping container," Jose informs me. "Found over two dozen women inside, some of them as young as fourteen."

"What did you do with the women?" I inquire.

"They're in our custody right now."

"Make sure they're fed and clothed before you turn them over to *Mano Amiga*. I bet a lot of the women are malnourished."

Even though I had threatened to turn Ramona over to a breeder, the truth is I hunt and kill sex traffickers. It's my one good deed for the world and which I do in honor of the only person I cared about. She lost a beloved cousin to a breeder and would weep anytime she read about human trafficking in the news. I'd walk through hell and back for her to shed one less tear.

Mano Amiga is a nonprofit of volunteers who help victims of human trafficking. I'm their biggest donor.

"What about the people transporting the women?" I ask.

"They're with *Diablo Viejo*, the Venezuelan cartel that recently ventured into breeding. We killed two of the five guys guarding the truck. What do you want me to do to the rest of them?"

"Execute them."

"You got it, boss."

I hand the phone back to Ming. Although I'm glad for the report from Jose, the truth is I could kill all the human traffickers in the world, and it still wouldn't atone for my wrongs.

After Ming leaves, I go back to Ramona and yank the last remaining clothespins off her arm, waist, and clit. She flinches ever so slightly.

"Cut her down and stick her in the chest," I tell Jack and Vlad.

For now, I'm done with her. But her present reprieve is only the calm before the storm. Tomorrow will be ten times worse.

CHAPTER NINE

MARTINA

MY BODY SORELY NEEDS a break from all the stimuli of pain. All I want is to be able to curl up in a corner somewhere and rest. Although my limbs welcome being released from their suspension, it's my mouth that is most grateful. My jaw is sore from being forced open, and I will never ever again under-appreciate saliva. I would die for a glass of water.

My wrists remain bound, and my ankles are shackled together before Jack lifts me and places me in some kind of storage chest. I try to fight him off but without success. When they close the top over me, I panic, worried that I'll run out of air being locked in the chest. Turns out there are small air holes, indicating the chest is intended to hold a breathing being. After they've locked the chest, I wait until I hear them leave before I push against the top.

I throw my shoulder against it, but the chest remains securely shut. Measuring about three feet by two feet, my cramped quarters prevent me from stretching out my limbs. At least I can be alone with my thoughts.

I wonder what Vincent was talking about on his phone call. If I didn't know him to be the ruthless leader of a triad capable of anything, I might have thought him someone trying to do good. He had mentioned what sounded like an organization with a Spanish name. *Manos amigas* sounds a lot like *manos amicas* in Italian, which translates to friendly or possibly helping hands.

I must not have the whole picture. The women he was talking about could be victims of human trafficking. Maybe Vincent is kidnapping them for his own nefarious purposes.

I close my eyes and try not to think about how much I crave a glass of water. How am I going to get out of here? And if I can't escape, how am I going to die as quickly as possible? If the saying "the good die young" is true, does its converse, that evil lives long, ring true as well? I still can't believe he dodged my bullet. Vincent Xu must be the luckiest bastard in the world.

I'll probably never get another shot at killing him. Shaking my head, I try to think more positively and review what I had observed about my surroundings. I saw only one door, only one way in, and the same way out. There're no windows. The vents are all too small for me to be able to fit through. There were some possible weapons, though. I saw canes and wooden paddles. They wouldn't make the best weapons, but beggars can't be choosers. I'm most interested in the pair of scissors. I'd like to jam those right between Vincent's eyes. I hate that he had his hands all over me and in my most intimate places. His moves are very deliberate, down to the fingertips. While it's true I haven't had sex in a while, there was a period in my life, shortly after losing my family, when all I did was alcohol, drugs, and sex. Most of the men I'd been with have pretty grubby paws for hands. But not Vincent. I wouldn't be surprised if he played the piano or something like that because his fingers are very controlled, capable of being gentle and punishing.

I'd like to crack his fingers one by one. But it wasn't his touch or the fact that he bared me naked before him and his goons that I found most degrading. It was having to lick his shoe. I had no choice, though.

I have heard the stories omegas tell about their experiences. One poor young omega male was powerless against his alpha rapist, and he couldn't even press charges. Well, he could, but his rapist had videotaped everything, including the parts where the omega begged for cock and ejaculated in his climax. No jury would believe it was nonconsensual sex. Most human beings, being neutral betas, don't understand the dynamics that go on between omegas and alphas.

I don't want to do anything Vincent wants, but if I don't have my omega blockers, my body will probably betray me. The one thing I won't give him, however, is my name. He seems to want to know who his killer is. I'll take that to my grave and let him wonder. Which of his enemies wants him dead? I know I'm not the only one. My contact on the inside, Brady Lee, has a vendetta against Vincent as well because Brady's fiancée, an omega, committed suicide after having slept with Vincent. Brady believes that Vincent took advantage of her being in heat. After her death, Brady reached out to a cousin who worked for the Black Dragon Triad.

His cousin got him a job working on Vincent's yacht.

Brady's on the yacht now, but we've kept our contact to a minimum. If anything goes wrong, we don't want to implicate each other. Brady is the closest thing I have to a friend at present. Ever since my family perished, I haven't bothered with friends and cut all my old ties. If there was a chance someone in my father's mafia betrayed us, I don't want them getting in the way of my objective to repay Vincent for the murder of my family.

Brady and I have been plotting this for over half a year. We've bonded over our shared mission. He's a decent guy, and if both of us weren't so messed up, we might have made a couple. Maybe. He's a little introspective for me, and I'm a little too emotional for him. So we're just friends. Friends with benefits. I mean, why not? We've both come to the conclusion that nothing's assured, and life's too short for most of us.

By now Brady probably knows I've failed in my attempt to kill Vincent. If I stand a chance of escaping or dying a quick death, I'm probably going to need Brady. I don't know if he's inclined to help me right now. I'm sure they're clamping down on security, and it's probably too risky for Brady to attempt anything.

But he's my only hope.

Chapter Ten

Vincent

As I sit in my office with its floor-to-ceiling windows looking out onto the sea, I run the other part of her name through my memory bank. Lazzarini. I don't know any Lazzarinis off the top of my head. It might be her married name, though she didn't have a reaction when I brought up the possibility of showing her degradation and torture to a significant other. It could also be a fake name, but I had Esen look into it anyway.

As if on cue, he enters my office and reports, "No Lazzarinis. No one by the name of Lazzarini has ever worked for you, no one by that name has ever partnered with you. Still working on friends and relatives of all Italians we've come across."

I lean back in my chair and steeple my thumbs and forefingers. "We're unlikely to find anything with extended friends or family. This is personal. I hurt her directly."

"I'll ask our Italian friends."

"Providing Lazzarini is her real name. And just because it happens to be Italian, don't confine your search to that."

"I know. I'm casting a wide net. Looking into everyone you've ever taken down. I also ran her prints and headshot. Nothing comes up. According to our FBI connect, she's not in any law enforcement database."

Something about this woman isn't adding up. I've only had good working relations with the mafia. The Aroldo family in Tampa is one of my distributors. They make bank from me and wouldn't have any reason to kill me.

"Any leads on who she might be working with?" I ask.

"We're quietly interviewing all the staff on board," Esen replies. "So far it seems she might have been working alone. Also, you have any directions on what to do with the body of Camellia and her bodyguards?"

"Not yet. Have Charlie and Margaret meet with me on that."

Margaret, a slender woman with a tomboy haircut and dramatic brows, arrives first and takes a chair in front of my desk.

"Charlie still messing around with pussy?" I ask.

She nods.

Charlie is a work hard, play hard type of person. It's worked for him, but playing at the extremes isn't balanced.

"Where's yours?" I ask Margaret of her girlfriend.

She raises her brows in surprise.

"You can't keep secrets from me," I say. "You should know that."

She looks down in guilt.

"She's very pretty," I remark. "Pretty name too. Daryna. Ukrainian?"

Margaret nods. "I was hoping to keep her as far from the Black Dragon as possible. She's an innocent."

At first I'm quiet. The pain that used to stab and twist my insides has quieted after three years, but it still flares, as it did when my would-be assassin gave me her name.

"I hate to break it to you," I finally say, "but you can't. If you want to keep her safe, you have to give her up."

"I thought about that," Margaret replies. "I guess I'm too selfish at the moment."

I nod. It's exactly how I was. Selfish. I didn't want to give up that which was most precious to me. As a result, I ended up with the worst possible outcome. The heavens punished me for my greed.

"You might get lucky," I tell Margaret. "But if you don't, will your present happiness be worth the future pain?"

Margaret is silent in thought when Charlie arrives.

"So what are we going to do about Camellia?" he asks. "We are conveniently out at sea, so we could sink her down to Davy Jones' locker."

"What was your goal in killing her?" Margaret asks.

This is another reason I'm leaning toward Margaret as my successor. She thinks big picture before zeroing in on the details.

"Payback," I reply. "The Ma Family Triad should know better than to mess with my turf."

"So should we send them pics of her dead body?" asks Charlie.

"It's probably torture enough for Old Man Ma to know that his only child is missing."

Camellia was slated to take over her father's position as head dragon of the Ma Family Triad. The loss for Ma will hit hard on many levels.

"If they know you killed her," Margaret notes, "they'll come after you hard, even though they've got to know there's no chance they win against us. Ma has too much pride not to seek vengeance for his daughter."

"But do they know we're behind Camellia's death?" Charlie asks.

"They'll suspect me for sure," I say, "but without evidence, Ma will have to stew in uncertainty. He's not rash enough to start a war on a hunch."

Getting Camellia onto my yacht had proved surprisingly easy. It hadn't been my intention initially to use her against her father. She and I happened to cross paths at a nightclub in Hong Kong. I pretended not to know who she was, even though she doesn't keep a low profile. She likes glamour and partying too much. She was partially drunk when hitting on the nightclub owner, a rich and handsome playboy named Caesar, but sober enough to issue a kill order. Another half drunk young woman in an even sexier outfit had insinuated herself onto Caesar's lap. The other woman crossed the line with Camellia when she spilled her drink onto Camellia and laughed instead of apologized.

I'm pretty good at reading lips, and from where I was sitting two tables over, I saw Camellia turn to one of her bodyguards and say, "I want this bitch dead."

A few minutes later, Caesar excused himself and went into one of the backrooms where he handles illicit business. Camellia said she was going to the ladies' room but instead went to speak to one of the club servers. I saw Camellia hand the woman several bills before heading toward the stairs. The server then went up to the young woman who had offended Camellia to say that Caesar would like her to join him upstairs in ten minutes.

When it was time, I followed the young woman upstairs, but by the time I reached the second floor, the hallway was empty.

I could hear, however, voices coming from one of the rooms. Pressing myself near the door, I could hear Camellia berating the young woman.

"You stupid bitch, you obviously don't know who I am. If you did, you wouldn't have spilled your fucking drink on me. And you didn't even apologize."

"Let me go!" the young woman said.

"Apologize!"

This was followed by the sound of a slap.

"Apologize, you bitch!"

"Jesus, I'm sorry!"

More slaps followed.

"Please! Stop! Let me go!" cried the woman.

"Too bad you're not going to live to regret what you did."

The sound of a gun, albeit muffled by a silencer, went off. That was when I decided to acquaint myself with Camellia.

"Do you want Ma to know it was you?" Margaret asks me.

"What do you think?" I ask.

"Once he knows it's you, we're going to have to take him out. Otherwise he'll be a continued nuisance."

Charlie lights up. "Let's do it. Let's capitalize on this opportunity."

"But if Vincent's goal is to make Old Man Ma suffer, then let him sweat it for a bit."

I voice my agreement. Charlie looks disappointed.

"You'll have your chance," I assure him before dismissing them.

Charlie and Margaret head out, but Margaret pauses on the threshold and turns to me.

"You ever lose someone you cared about?" she asks. "Someone who wasn't in the business?"

The vision of my Irene as she lay upon her apartment floor, covered in blood as she drew her last breaths, flashes through my mind.

Twelve bullets. Between the two of them, the killers put twelve fucking bullets into her. With a slight and delicate build, she probably wouldn't have survived a single bullet. She was still alive when I found her. But I was too late.

She died in my arms.

Along with our unborn child.

Looking at Margaret, I answer, "The trick is not to care about anyone in that way. Then you don't have to worry about losing them."

*****

The following morning, I wake up early. I feel unsettled. Probably not surprising given I just survived an attempt on my life. But that's only partially it.

After my morning tea, I have my second set of bodyguards, Reggie and Cho, follow me to the dungeon. I instruct them to haul "Ramona" out of the trunk. I half expect her to fight against my men, but her limbs must be sore from spending hours in the cramped confines. And she probably knows resisting would be a waste of her energy. She has half circles under her eyes, so I doubt she got much quality sleep in that trunk.

They set her on her knees.

"Sleep well?" I ask to rub it in. "Hungry? Thirsty?"

She looks up at the last question. Her lips are cracked, and not just because they suffered a good cut. They're a plump pair. I bet they'd look pretty wrapped around my cock.

I direct Cho to get a bottle of water, then squat down to look her in the eyes. "This is how today is going to work: I ask you a question, and you answer. If I like your answer, you get rewarded. If I don't, you get punished."

She stares at me without fear. I didn't expect her to be afraid. Yet.

I pose the first question. "Who are you working with?"

"What do I get for my answer?" she asks.

Cho hands me a glass bottle of premium water. I pop the cap off with my thumb and hold the bottle before her.

She eyes it ravenously before saying, "No one. I work alone."

I wait a beat before placing the bottle at my lips and taking a drink. Her mouth hangs agape as she watches me.

I swallow loudly and reply, "Bullshit."

"I'm a loner," she explains. "And I don't need anyone. They'll only get in the way."

"Hard to believe you could get cleared as an employee without someone on the inside helping you out. So who is it?"

When she doesn't answer, I take another drink. A long one.

"I said no one," she insists.

I take another long gulp. The bottle is now half empty.

She stares at the remaining water with a frown. "You should just skip straight to the punishment if you're not going to believe a word I say."

She speaks with conviction, so I contemplate the possibility that maybe she is working alone. But that would mean she could hack into our database to designate herself an employee, which would also have required her to pass Esen's security screening first. That's a lot to accomplish.

I stand up. "If you say so, pet."

CHAPTER ELEVEN

MARTINA

SHIT. I'D PROBABLY BE better off if Vincent had just killed me already. Instead, I have to endure his sadism. How do people like this stuff? Are they all masochists? Or maybe I'm just not experienced or adventurous enough with sex. But I don't think what Vincent is doing qualifies as BDSM because I'm guessing with consensual kink, there's an element of pleasure for both parties. What Vincent is doing is strictly torture, and it's for his benefit only. And I have to endure this for how many days before I die? If my limbs are always going to be bound, my chances of escape are next to nil. I can't just wait and hope that an opportunity will present itself. Vincent is too shrewd to let that happen. I also can't rely on Brady, who may or may not assume that Vincent's goons have already thrown me over the side of the yacht. And even if Brady knew I was alive, would he risk himself to save me?

"Fetch me the potted nettle from the sunroom," says Vincent before turning back to me. "You sure you don't want to give me a name?"

With Cho gone, there's only two of them. I wonder if there is a way to get it down to just one man. It still won't be easy, but the odds would be much better.

I look Vincent in the eyes and contemplate giving him a fake name, like I did with mine, but what if I accidentally implicate someone innocent?

"There's no name to give you," I answer. "And even if I did give you a name, would you believe me? Or would you just torture me anyway, for the fun of it?"

"That's an interesting thought, and I should absolutely torture you just for the fun of it. But, believe it or not, I'm a man of my word. If you tell me the truth, and not some bullshit, I'll spare you the punishment I have in mind."

"What punishment is that?"

He gives me a smile, like he's indulging a child. "If you're not going to cooperate, you'll find out soon enough. What you see–"

He sweeps his arm toward all the different implements and apparatuses in the room.

"–is just some of the ways I can inflict pain."

You've already inflicted the worst possible pain.

He seems to read my mind and says, "I don't know you from Adam right now, but I'm going to find out who you are, where you came from, who your loved ones are. You wouldn't want them to pay a price for your crimes, would you?"

Ha! I have no loved ones thanks to you!

"Maybe I should let you live long enough to bear witness to their demise."

I stare at him hard. "You're one evil, messed up son of a bitch."

"I know. But why should I be anything else when good, innocent people suffer every day, when they're slaughtered for doing nothing but love–"

For a second, he seems to have slipped into a different world. I never expected the words "innocent" and "love" to be in his vocabulary.

Rousing himself, he shakes off his momentary lapse into humanity and narrows his eyes at me. "It's actually better that you don't cooperate. Gives me a reason to punish you even more."

"Like you need one."

He grins in amusement and taps me playfully on the nose. "Cute. You normally this snarky in your dying days?"

I want to tell him that if he touches my nose again, I'll bite his finger off. "What do I have to lose?"

"Peace. Dignity. Comfort. You tell me everything I want to know, I'll let you die a relatively quick and pain-free death. Otherwise, your last days will be filled with misery, pain, and humiliation."

"And why would I believe you would do anything remotely nice? Because you're a 'man of your word'?"

"You think I could've gotten as far as I have by being someone who can't be trusted?"

"It happens all the time. Just look at the politicians, the billionaires in this world. Everywhere you turn, some asshole succeeds. And they aren't even the criminals. At least not legally. Maybe morally. But instead of getting their just due, they're rewarded, even idolized."

"I'm in agreement with you there, pet. It shows you there's no real morality, no justice. Maybe in the afterlife. But for the present, why try to be good when you can get fucked over anyway? As the saying goes, nice guys finish last."

While he and I both see that one can be an asshole and still get ahead, I don't know that I'm ready to draw the same conclusion that he has. Nice guys don't always finish last. At least that's what I want to believe. Only it isn't panning out in my case.

"That being said," Vincent continues, "I believe that backstabbing and chronic dishonesty are only short-term strategies to success. And it tends to attract similar people, equally self-interested and untrustworthy. It doesn't inspire genuine loyalty."

I can't imagine someone as ruthless as Vincent Xu having anything close to principles. If he does, it's only because they're self-serving and happens to coincide with what's right.

Cho returns holding a large potted plant with several stems. I've never seen a nettle plant before. It's about three feet tall with dark green, heart-shaped leaves.

"I passed by Ming on the way here," Cho says to Vincent. "He says Anh Nguyen called. Wants to pitch an idea to you."

Vincent goes over to the chest of drawers and pulls out a pair of leather gloves. "Nguyen is into human trafficking. I don't deal with traffickers."

Why not? I wonder. Don't tell me there's actually a bar that Vincent won't go beneath.

"He's the worst kind of trafficker too," Vincent continues as he slips on the gloves.

"Yeah?" Cho asks.

"Nguyen traffics children. His so-called travel agencies help connect men from Western countries with prepubescent girls in Thailand and Malaysia. He's made bank because there's no shortage of men from places like the US who'll pay good money to stick their prick into some poor little girl. If I ever come across Nguyen, I'll kill him personally on the spot."

This is not a side of Vincent I ever expected to see. I thought he didn't see any sense in being 'good,' so why does he care about what this Nguyen guy does? And Vincent didn't give a shit about killing a kid as young as my brother. Don't tell me Vincent grew a conscience in recent years. I don't believe that's possible.

As if reading my mind again, Vincent tells me, "I'm not going to try and convince you of anything about me. You can tell me what I want to know, and maybe I'll spare you extra punishment, and maybe I won't. You can't know for sure, but it's your choice whether or not you want to roll the dice and find out."

For a moment, I weigh my options. But I'm not giving up Brady. I know that if I'm not successful at killing Vincent, Brady will try, and maybe he'll succeed where I haven't. There's no guarantee I can give Vincent an answer he'll believe anyway, so I stick with my strategy of pretending that I'm working alone. "If I had someone helping me, don't you think I'd give them up by now? Knowing I'm going to die one way or the other?"

Vincent studies me.

"Trust me, I'm not that noble," I add.

"If you're not telling the truth, then you're a pretty good liar," he seems to think aloud. "If you are telling the truth, then you're unlucky."

He tells his men to secure me to the six-foot-tall bondage post while he cuts two stalks of the nettle. My arms remain pinioned behind me as Reggie wraps my neck with rope and Cho ties my ankles to the post behind me.

Holding the nettle, which has fine hairs on its stems and leaves, in his gloved hand, Vincent stands in front of me. "You're welcome to give up your partner in crime at any point to stop the punishment. Like I said, I'll eventually find out who they are anyway."

"I would! If there was anyone to give up," I insist.

Whack!

The nettle whips the side of my breast. At first I don't feel anything other than the impact, but the sting sets in about ten seconds after, increasing in intensity after he strikes the same area several more times. He does the same to my other breast. After several minutes, the sting turns into a burn. Round wheals appear over my skin.

"I once made a sub bathe in a tub of nettles," Vincent says while flogging my belly and legs. "I even shoved some into her cunt."

My eyes grow wide. The poor woman!

"She was a painslut, so she loved it," he says. "Are you a painslut, pet?"

I don't respond, but inwardly, I'm shaking my head vociferously. The nettles hurt, but I can take it. Having them inside me, though?

"How about we fill your cunt with nettle, then follow that up with some fisting with the nettle still inside you?"

I blanch. That sounds absolutely horrible.

He brushes the nettle over a nipple. Part of me wants to stifle my reaction because I'm sure he delights in my visible suffering, and I don't want to give him that satisfaction. But if I don't react enough, will that push him to go harder on me?

"How are your nipples doing?" he asks before swatting at them with the nettles.

I refrain from wincing. I'm not sure what answer is best for me. Should I admit they're sore?

Not waiting for my response, he says, "I have just the thing for them."

Dread fills me as I watch him head to an armoire and pull out a contraption with two metal plates with little spikes facing each other. A tree-like accessory, with what looks like nipple clamps dangling from the limbs, juts out from the middle. This thing does not look friendly.

He hands it to Cho, explaining, "This is a breast press. Ever play around with breast torture?"

"You're such a sick fuck," I tell him.

"Thank you. Believe it or not, there are plenty of subs who enjoy this kind of stuff. Who knows, maybe you will too."

It's not impossible, but with Vincent, never.

"Put it on her," he tells Cho.

Cho traps my breasts between the steel plates and turns the screws that will make the plates squish my breasts. I tell myself this is probably no different than getting a mammogram.

But a mammogram machine doesn't have teeth!

My breasts flatten into a distorted shape. If Cho keeps going, the spikes will puncture into my breasts. I clench my jaw and try not to whine.

"Now add the nipple stretching," Vincent directs.

Cho applies the clamps to my nipples and slides the bar along the shaft. The further it gets from me, the more it pulls on my nipples.

"More," Vincent says when Cho stops.

I can't contain my whimpers. I thoroughly hate having nipples now. Yes, I usually like some attention to them during sex, but I can do without them.

Cho steps aside to let Vincent admire the effect. Vincent wiggles one of the nipple clamps. I grit my teeth.

"Anything you want to share, pet?"

That if you give me the chance, I'll tear your nipples off and have them for breakfast.

"No? Well, we have plenty of time," Vincent says. "We're just getting started."

He whips me a couple of times with the nettle, but the pain is nothing compared to what my poor breasts and nipples are enduring. The flattened orbs are turning purple.

What feels like an eternity later but is probably no more than fifteen or twenty minutes, Vincent orders Cho to remove the breast presser.

"We don't want her tits rotting just yet," Vincent explains.

I draw in a ragged breath when my breasts are freed. But now I have a different problem.

I need to pee.

Chapter Twelve

Vincent

S HE DOES HER BEST to contain her squirming, but I can tell her thighs are clamped tightly together. "Something the matter?"

At first, she just keeps her gaze down without a word.

"Nothing? Then let's proceed with the punishment," I say.

"I need to pee," she blurts.

I let her predicament marinate while I contemplate how much indignity and discomfort I want to force on her. I've done a good amount, but apparently not enough. She hasn't broken. Instead, she's trying her best to be stoic, to pretend like she doesn't feel the pain. For what? Just to deny me the satisfaction of seeing her suffer?

She's more intriguing than I expected.

I'm not that noble, she said. So why is she holding back on giving up whoever helped her? Is she possibly telling the truth that she's doing this all on her own?

Why am I starting to question myself? As smart and capable as she might be, it's not easy to get past my security. And she has to have a breaking point. I'll get to it eventually. In the meantime, the sadist in me is having fun. Her tits looked fucking amazing trapped in the breast presser. They're losing their purple hue now but are still crimson from the rash the nettles gave her.

Cutting into the silence, she asks, "Is there somewhere I can...? I doubt you want me to relieve myself all over your floor."

I give her a reassuring smile. "Oh, I don't mind. I'll just make you clean it up. Maybe the same way you cleaned my floor yesterday."

She looks horrified.

I tell Cho to untie her, then push her down to her knees.

"Tell you what," I say. "Why don't you help Reggie with his hard-on first, then I'll let you take a piss."

Her frown deepens while Reggie smiles. He adjusts his crotch in anticipation.

"Go on," I urge her. "The sooner you get him to come, the sooner you can answer nature's call."

After a moment's hesitation, she wiggles her way over to him on her knees. Reggie, grinning from ear to ear, unzips his pants and pulls out his cock, which is semi-erect and already a good length. She stares at it with misgiving, but she parts her lips and takes him into her mouth.

"Oh man," Reggie groans.

I take care of the men who work my security detail, but they've never received a perk like this.

I can't tell if she's practiced at giving blowjobs or not. Because her mouth is dry, she doesn't slide smoothly over Reggie's cock, but that doesn't mean it's not pleasurable for him.

"You're not taking enough of him, pet," I say as I approach them. Placing my hand on the back of her head, I push her further down his length. She gags but adjusts.

"A little more," I urge as I continue to press her head down.

She chokes, but I hold her in place. Her body starts to heave as she tries to dislodge Reggie's cock from her throat. After it looks like she might turn blue in the face, I let her come off of him to catch her breath. She coughs. It must make her want to pee even more because she clamps her legs together even tighter.

"You better get back up on that cock," I tell her.

She takes my advice and quickly goes back to swallowing Reggie. Though it must not feel good with that cut on her lip, she wraps her mouth snugly over Reggie's shaft. She sucks him in earnest, her cheeks caving inward with the effort.

"Oh man," Reggie moans. "Is it okay if I come, boss?"

"Sure," I reply, "but take your time."

At that, she seems determined to take as much of Reggie as possible.

"Damn that feels good," he grunts and says after several minutes, "I don't think I can hold off much longer."

To her, I say, "I know you're thirsty, so you better drink up every last drop of Reggie's cum."

Reggie closes his eyes. His body trembles. His hips buck, and his cock almost pops out of her mouth. With a loud grunt, Reggie shoots his load into her. Either she's not ready or she doesn't like the taste of his cum because she spits most of it out. Some of it lands on her thighs, and some of it lands on the floor.

Taking a knee beside her, I push her head to the ground. "I said to drink every last drop."

After she slurps the cum off the floor, I gather what's on her thighs with my forefinger and push the rest into her mouth.

"I want to feel you swallow it," I say.

I feel her tongue pressing my finger to the roof of her mouth as she does, then I feel her pulling away. I get the feeling she'd rather have Reggie's cock than my finger in her mouth, so I jam my middle finger into her mouth. I shove them deep enough for her to choke. Her eyes widen. She stops resisting. The urge to pee must've gotten stronger. She turns her gaze to me, asking if she can go.

The answer is no.

"Wouldn't be fair to Cho if we left him out," I explain.

Reggie moves aside for Cho to take his place. Cho pulls out his cock and traces the outline of her lips with the tip.

"Think you can last longer than Reggie?" I ask him.

"Sure," he answers.

I hand her over to him. He grabs her hair and guides her slowly up and down his cock. At one point he pushes her down far enough that his pubes tickle her nose. She tries her best not to gag and mostly succeeds.

"She's really dry," Cho says after several minutes.

I hand him the bottle of water, which he pours over his cock. Ravenously, she descends on his cock, trying to slurp up every last drop of the precious liquid. When she comes off his cock, hoping to get the water directly into her mouth, he stops. Only when she gets back on does he start splashing the water between his cock and her mouth. I've never seen a woman suck cock so voraciously before. Heat churns in my loins.

After all the water is gone, she still has an incentive to give Cho the best head he's ever had. She resumes her sucking and tries to accelerate her motions, but with his grasp of her hair, Cho still commands the pace. She tries another tactic, moaning into his cock as if she can't get enough of him. The addition of sound seems to work. I see Cho's brow furrow. I feel my own body responding.

She adds purring and panting. Cho's lashes flutter. He's trying to hold off, but it looks like she might be doing something with her tongue. Soon, I see the muscles of his face tense. With a groan, he presses his pelvis into her face as he comes. This time she swallows the cum without letting a drop fall.

When she comes off him, she can barely turn to me. Her focus is on her bladder. Maybe she's worried she's going to make a mess on the floor, and I'll make her lick it up. I'm a messed up fucker, so I can't say I won't consider it. My cock is pretty stiff from watching her blow Cho and Reggie. Even if she didn't need to piss, she wouldn't want to suck my cock. Requiring her to do so would make her writhe in misery, which is my aim.

Adjusting my crotch, I step toward her.

CHAPTER THIRTEEN

MARTINA

S HIT. HE'S GOING TO *move the goalposts again. The fucker. And there's nothing I can do about it.*

I see Vincent adjust his crotch before he starts coming toward me. He's got a hard-on, and he's going to make me take care of him. Knowing him, he's going to make the blowjob last as long as possible. There's no way I can hold my pee any longer. It's taking every fiber in my body not to release it. My body is fighting itself.

I stare at Vincent's crotch. Which is worse: pissing myself in front of three grown men or sucking off the man I hate the most in the world?

It doesn't matter what the answer is because my bladder can't take the pressure anymore. I feel a dribble come out, and there's no way I can hold the dam. The urine gushes out of me. The relief is so, so sweet.

But when it's all over, I feel my cheeks burn. Suddenly, I'm transported to when I was four years old and wet my bed because I had drank two glasses of chocolate milk before going to bed—something I wasn't supposed to do. My mother was upset, and I was mortified.

I expect Vincent to tell me how disgusting I am, how dirty to be kneeling in my own piss. Next he'll want me to lick it all up, like I had to with the omega blocker and Reggie's cum.

"You're going to have to clean that mess up," Vincent says.

I seethe. If he had let me go when I needed to, this accident wouldn't have happened. But he wants me in pain and misery. And he's succeeding. I would take more of the breast and nipple torture over this, though. This humiliation.

"Get her a mop," Vincent directs the guy named Cho. "When she's done mopping the floor, stick her in the cage. Get her a bucket in case she needs to go again."

I watch Vincent walk away, followed by his men. Is he not going to force me to blow him?

When the door closes behind them, my relief is almost as great as what I felt when I finally got to empty my bladder. My thirst is still poignant, however. The water I was able to slurp off of Cho's dick was less refreshing after he filled my mouth with tangy cum. I wonder if there's any way I can get more of that water.

"Hard to clean the floor with my hands bound behind my back," I tell Cho when he returns with a bucket of soapy water and a mop.

"Try," he replies. "Vincent will be down later to inspect the cleaning job."

When I get to my feet, I can feel my piss trickle down the insides of my leg. I manage to grasp the mop from Cho. He lights a cigarette while watching me mop the floor. What I would really like to clean is myself.

"You have any paper towels?" I ask.

"Nope."

"Can I get some?"

"Nope."

So you're just as much an asshole as your boss.

Mopping with my hands behind my back isn't as hard as I thought it would be. When I'm done, Cho grabs my arm and hauls me over to a cage that looks like it's meant for a medium- to large-sized dog.

He pushes me down to my knees.

"Get in," he directs.

For a moment, I wonder if I can take him, but I quickly nix the idea. Even if I manage to kick him and knock him down somehow, I wouldn't get very far with my ankles and wrists bound. I at least need some way to free my hands. It would be great if Cho had a knife on him.

"Go," he orders, giving me a light shove with his foot.

I hobble into the cage on my knees. He shuts the cage door behind me and locks it. After he leaves, I assess my situation. The cage has more room than the trunk but isn't a lot more comfortable. I wish my body would go numb so I wouldn't feel how my breasts are tender, my ass stings, and my ribs ache. I want water to wash away my thirst and the taste of Reggie and Cho's cum. I want a shower too, to cleanse the urine from me. Staring at the bucket that serves as my chamber pot, I start to feel a little defeated.

No. I'm not going out that way. I'm not giving that son of a bitch the satisfaction. I'm going to go down kicking. This isn't over until I'm dead. And if there's any way of taking Vincent with me, that's a victory.

I notice that the pair of scissors Jack had used the other day is still on top of the chest of drawers. If I could get to that...and if I could find a way to communicate with Brady...

Spent, I lay down on my side and consider taking a nap. If Vincent wants to torture me in all ways possible, he'll add sleep deprivation, so I should use this opportunity to get some rest.

Luckily, I manage to sleep for what feels like several hours before I hear the door open. The unlucky part is I feel my body buzzing in an abnormal way because I haven't had my daily dose of omega blockers.

Chapter Fourteen

Vincent

OVER THE VIDEO STREAM, I watch as she does a good job mopping the floor clean. Either she's thorough or she's worried she might have to clean up any missed spots with her tongue. I could have had her blow me while sitting in her own piss. It would have been nice to relieve the wood I had. I'm not sure why I didn't. And that doesn't sit well with me.

It's not that I need to satisfy myself every time I'm aroused. It's that I saw a brief crack in her armor, and I didn't try to bust that crack wide open. I should have reveled in the sick look on her face when I approached her. I could tell what was going on in her mind. She was worried she'd have to suck my cock next. And she would probably rather jump off a cliff than blow me. It's probably just as well I didn't go through with it because she'd probably try to bite my dick off.

But I could have made her lick the floor clean after she couldn't hold it anymore. Instead, I lost my ruthlessness.

But I'll make that up when I see her next.

In the meantime, I meet with Rusakov, the head of a Bratva based in Europe. They're trying but not succeeding with a concoction that would enable betas to mimic alpha characteristics. I already know they don't have the capabilities for this type of product development, whereas I have the connections to some of the best scientists in the US and China, but what Rusakov is good at is cyber blackmail, so it's worth a talk.

After our meeting, I take a swim in the pool on the main deck. As I warm up, it occurs to me that she—my Irene—would find it hard to believe that I could own my own pool, let alone one on a luxury yacht built specifically to my specs. Thanks to the production of omega blockers, an effort I pushed for, I'm filthy, stinking rich.

But she isn't here to share it with me.

I'd give it all away in an instant if I could bring her back. She wouldn't care for this kind of shit anyway. I bet if she had the kind of money I had now, she'd still want to live in nothing larger than a two-bedroom apartment in Guilin. I was the one who wanted more for her. It was why I didn't leave the triad right away. I wanted to stick around long enough to make bank before I pulled out.

And I will never forgive myself for my mistake.

Fuck.

Why are these thoughts invading me? I thought I was done with them, but apparently they've just been hiding in the shadows.

I start to swim faster, pounding the water, going until my muscles are on fire and it hurts to breathe.

Esen is waiting for me when I get out.

After I catch my breath, he informs me, "Got a list of deaths that the Cosa Nostra put together for us. They went back ten years. I can ask them to go back further if you'd like."

Toweling off, I take the list from him and scan the names. No Lazzarinis. But that doesn't mean my assassin isn't affiliated with anyone on the list. Most of the names are not familiar to me. One, however, does stand out to me.

Rossi.

They're Miami mafia. I had thought to partner with them to help distribute my omega blockers to the southeast portion of the United States.

That fell through after Luca Rossi was killed. I chose to work with a different mafia, the Aroldos, based in Tampa. I suspect the Aroldos had something to do with the massacre of the family, but I couldn't get proof. The cops had even less to go on than I did.

I hand the list back to Esen. "There's no obvious connection that I can see."

"I have all our Italian connects looking into the name Irene Lazzarini, but they've found nothing so far."

"Keep at it, but as I've said before, don't confine your research to Italians."

"I know, boss."

Sitting down on one of the lounge chairs, I breathe in the warm, salty air while the Lazzarini name repeats in my head. It's like this woman came out of nowhere. Aside from Old Man Ma, I'm not beefing with anyone and haven't in the last two years. I get the feeling that following the Italian thread will lead to a dead end. I've never had issues with any mafia before. The mob, or Irish mafia, yes, but I've only been on good terms with the Italians.

I shouldn't let it bother me that I don't have the answers, but it does. Something about this Ramona bitch irritates me. Especially since she's disturbed the dust of old memories. I want it to stop.

Time to pay "pet" another visit.

*****

She must be very tired because my entering does not wake her. I sit in a chair and motion for Jack to set down the dish of water on the table beside me. He and Vlad, the security team that has the late-night shift, stand several feet behind me while I watch her sleep. I have resolved not to be so nice with her this time around.

She sleeps curled on her side, her lips slightly parted. The rash on her breasts hasn't completely disappeared yet.

Though she might bear the same name as the angel who was brutally ripped from my life, she bears few similarities to my Irene. My Irene had a slender and petite figure. With her jet-black hair and light complexion, she would've made the perfect actress for Snow White. She was a living Disney princess in that she was pure of heart and full of compassion. Who else would've loved a godforsaken soul like me? My Irene was a delicate orchid I wanted to cherish and protect. Only I failed her. I failed her miserably.

This Irene with her darker olive complexion, thicker thighs, supple hips, and piercing eyes is more like a cactus. She's a survivor despite her tough environment. But even cactuses can wither and die.

Tired of waiting, I tell Vlad to go wake her up. He walks over and roughly kicks the cage. She wakens in an instant.

"Dinner time," I tell her, then nod at Vlad.

He undoes his belt and unbuttons his pants. After unzipping, he pulls out his cock and wiggles it at her.

"Sit up and take your meal like a good pet," I command.

She glares at me.

"If you do a good job, I have something for you," I say before taking the dish of water and setting it down on the floor for her to see.

At that, she gets on her knees. Vlad sticks his cock through the cage. She parts her lips and takes him into her mouth.

"Good pet," I praise.

There isn't the urgency she had earlier when giving fellatio to Reggie and Cho, but she's plenty thirsty still and earnestly slides her mouth over Vlad's shaft. I can tell it's not the most comfortable angle for Vlad to be pressing his pelvis against the side of the cage, so I tell him to let her out.

"Let Jack in on some of the fun," I say after Vlad unlocks the cage and pulls her out.

"Wait," I order before he shoves his cock back into her mouth.

Getting up, I go over to the chest of drawers and select a plain leather collar with a chain leash. I want to add insult to injury wherever I can. I walk over to her. "A good pet needs a good collar."

She balks and shies away from the collar.

"Hold her," I instruct Vlad.

He grabs the hair at the top of her head while I clasp the collar around her neck.

I pat her cheek. "That's a good little bitch."

She looks ready to bite my head off. I bet she'd prefer that I punch her instead of having to wear the demeaning collar.

"Continue," I tell Jack and Vlad.

They stand on either side of her with their cocks pointed at her face. She doesn't like either of them. Of the five men and one woman who make up my security detail, Cho and Reggie from earlier are the nicest of the six, and Jack and Vlad are the meanest.

"If you can't decide who to suck off first, then take both of them," I suggest.

She doesn't budge.

I nudge the dish with the toe of my shoe. A little bit of water splashes out. "You want your water, don't you?"

Reluctantly, she opens her mouth. Jack and Vlad angle their cocks into her open orifice, stretching her lips.

Damn that looks hot.

My guys piston their cocks in and out of her mouth. At one point, Vlad takes himself out and whacks his cock against her cheek. He tries to shove it into one of her nostrils. I shake my head. The asshole. But I'm also slightly amused.

Next he aims his cock at her eye. She shirks away, coming off Jack.

"Dude," Jack complains.

"All right, all right," Vlad says.

She wraps her mouth fully around Jack, but Vlad isn't content to rub his cock and wait. He pokes it at her, annoying her.

"Let me have a turn," Vlad says before pulling her off Jack and turning her head toward his own crotch.

She hesitates.

"It's his cock or mine," I tell her.

She parts her mouth and takes him. Vlad bucks himself roughly into her mouth, at times pushing the tip of his cock into her cheek as if he wanted to make it come out the other side.

"Don't forget about Jack," I say.

Vlad shoves her off him, and she goes back to blowing Jack.

"She any good?" I ask him.

"Not bad," he answers. "But I've had better."

"Something to work toward then, pet," I direct to her.

"Could use some lube. Her mouth's dry as shit."

"How is shit dry?" Vlad asks.

"You get what I mean, fucker."

"Here. I'll help you out. Give her to me." Vlad takes Jack's place and jerks himself. "Open your mouth, bitch."

She frowns, glances at the dish of water, and does what he says.

Aiming his cock at her mouth, he comes. His cum spurts into her mouth. But he's not done. He squeezes out another glob, which he shoots at her eye. Some of it runs down her cheek, and the rest sits on her lashes. Vlad cleans his cock off on her other cheek. She spits out his cum, which dribbles down her chin and drops to her chest.

"That's some disgusting shit," she says.

For all his macho exterior, Vlad is thin-skinned. He makes a move like he's going to punch her.

"Hey," I bark, not because I care whether or not he hits her, but because I haven't given him permission to do so.

Vlad puts his fist down and mutters, "Stupid slut."

Ready for his turn to come, Jack pulls her back toward him.

"Now your junk's going to be on my cock," Jack says to Vlad.

"At least she's not dry anymore," Vlad replies.

Jack stuffs his cock back into her mouth. She sucks him off, looking like an amateur porn actor. Maybe she's trying to make it good for Jack to piss Vlad off. She also probably wants this all to be over with so that she can have her water.

But I've got a surprise for her.

CHAPTER FIFTEEN

MARTINA

I work Jack's cock good because I want that dish of water. And because I want Vlad to see what he is missing out on by being such a dick. I hate that his cum is all over me.

"She's gotten better already, boss," Jack says to Vincent.

Rolling his hips, Jack matches my rhythm.

"That's it, bitch, that's it!" he exclaims as his thrusts quicken.

His body stiffens as he climaxes. Halfway through spilling his cum into my mouth, he pulls out so that the rest hits my chest. He stumbles back. Vlad grabs my hair with one hand while the other rubs the cum over a breast. He has big, grubby hands. If I'm still alive after killing Vincent, I'm going for Vlad next. I imagine cutting off his cock and sticking it into his mouth.

After Vlad releases me, I look over at the dish of water. Vincent doesn't overlook much in the way of details. He could've given me the water in a glass, but no, he's going to make me lap the water out of a dish like I'm his pet dog.

Seeing my gaze, Vincent says, "One more thing."

I should've known he'd move the goalposts yet again. What does he want now?

"Before you get to have the water, tell me your name again."

I stare at him, trying to contain how much I hate this man.

"Pet," I answer.

At that, he laughs. "Clever. What's my name?"

Lots of different words come to mind, but I want that water, so I respond, "Stronzo."

"*Master* Stronzo."

Whatever, you mother-fucking piece of shit.

"Say it correctly."

The childish part of me doesn't want to do anything he tells me, but that won't get me anywhere, so I mutter, "Master Stronzo."

"Now give me the name you were born with."

"M—Irene Lazzarini."

His eyes narrow at my near mistake. Maybe I should give him my real name, though I also want to save it for the moment right before he dies. Given that he had my whole family killed, I'm surprised he hasn't guessed who I might be. Granted, no one knew I made it out alive. A neighbor found me before the cops arrived. He knew my father was in the business and took me to his house. I stayed there till my grandmother arrived and took me away. I firmly believe my grandmother died of a broken heart, so that's on Vincent as well.

I would have expected Vincent to have come up with the Rossi name by now. Maybe he knows too many Italians to count or has killed so many people that my family is just a small blip on his radar.

"You were about to say something other than Irene," he remarks.

"I was going to say 'Master Stronzo,'" I reply, grimacing while I pronounce his 'name.'

Vincent walks over and grabs my cheeks.

Can you see how much I hate you? I ask with my eyes.

"Next question," he says slowly. "Who's your connect? Who got you onto my yacht?"

"I already told you," I say as his grip presses harder into my face. "I did it myself."

He shakes his head and releases me. Standing up, he goes over to the dish of water.

"Try again," he says.

Oh no.

My stomach grumbles, but water is what I want most. Still, I can't throw Brady under the bus.

"I didn't work with anyone," I insist.

Vincent considers my answer, then kicks the dish over. I watch as that delicious liquid spills onto the floor.

"Either you forgot that each time you lie, you get punished," he says, "or you're awfully loyal to this person. Or persons. The thing is, pet, I'm going to find out one way or another. So you're not helping yourself at all. And maybe not the person you're protecting either. Because the longer it takes me to find them, the more pissed off I'll be. And I'm the kind of guy who takes his anger out on others."

Turning to his men, he orders them to lock me in the pillory. They drag me over to the wooden apparatus. Even though I know it probably won't do any good, I fight them. When Jack grabs my arms from behind, I leverage his body to push myself up and kick at Vlad.

"Fucking bitch!" he spits. "She almost got me in the balls again!"

They bend my body ninety degrees to fit the device. As Vlad holds my neck down, Jack frees my wrists so that he can put them in place beside my head.

They close the pillory over me, locking me into the holes for my neck and wrists. Vincent approaches holding two implements. One is a wooden paddle about half an inch thick, covered in holes. The other is some kind of rattan or bamboo cane about 8mm in diameter. He hands each man an implement. "Jack, you get the paddle. Vlad, you get the cane."

Vlad smirks at me. Shit. I shouldn't have kicked him.

Threading his fingers through my hair, Vincent yanks my head back. "We're going to play a little game. I'm going to ask you a question. If I don't feel like you're telling me the truth, you're going to get a spanking."

When he releases me, I drop my head and stare at the floor. I hear him walk back to the chest of drawers. He brings back a small metallic device with two hooks. It looks like it might belong at the end of a fishing line. After securing twine to the top, to my dismay, he hooks the two prongs of the device into my nostrils. He wraps the twine around the pillory behind my head. This forces my head back unless I want the hooks ripping through my nostrils.

He pulls his chair over and sits down in front of me. "Now we can begin the game. First question: how many people are you working with?"

He knows I'm not working alone, but if I back down on this question, he has even more reason not to trust any answer I give him.

"I told you before," I say. "I'm not working with anyone, surprisingly, because I bet there are dozens of people who want to kill you."

"That's insulting," he says placidly. "I would've thought at least a hundred, not mere dozens. Your answer is unsatisfactory."

Looking up at Jack and Vlad, he nods. I feel the whack of the wooden paddle against my ass, the force of it sending my shoulders into the pillory. The nose hooks pull at my nostrils. Before I can fully register the blow, Vlad strikes me with the cane.

"You'll have to tell me, when this is all over, whether you prefer a stinging pain or a setting pain," Vincent says. "I'm going to assume you're working with at least one other person, someone who helped you get into the employee database. I want you to think carefully before answering my next question because each time I think you're lying to me, I'm going to double the number of spanks. Is your contact aboard my yacht right now?"

"There isn't anybody else," I insist, hoping that he might start to believe me if I'm consistent.

"Not a good answer," Vincent says before nodding at his men.

Whump! Whump!

I feel like Jack is trying to break my ass with the paddle.

Whip! Whip!

And it feels like Vlad is trying to cut into my buttocks with the cane.

"Is the connect a man or a woman?" Vincent asks.

"There is no connect," I reiterate.

He shakes his head at me. "Now we're at four with the paddle and four with the cane."

God have mercy.

The paddle is unforgiving as it connects with my derrière, but the cane is almost worse, probably because Vlad is doing his best to get back at me for kicking him in the balls.

Getting up from his chair, Vincent lifts my chin and looks into my eyes. "Whoever you're protecting, I hope they're worth it because your poor ass is paying no small price."

He releases my chin and goes to stand behind me. I feel his hand on a buttock, gently caressing the bruised and smarting flesh.

Oh fuck.

My body reacts. Not in a good way. At least not what I consider good.

This can't be happening.

I'm less than twenty-four hours away from my missed dose and already my omega traits are kicking in? Or maybe it has something to do with Vincent and how close he's standing to me. Like I'm picking up on his pheromones. Because even though his touch stings, I can feel my body growing warm.

Fuck. Fuck. Fuck.

CHAPTER SIXTEEN

VINCENT

INTERESTING. HER BODY SEEMED to melt right before it stiffened beneath my touch. I continue caressing the angry red slash marks of the cane layered over the deep pink of the paddle. If she had been a true submissive of mine and one relatively new to BDSM, I would have gone with a much slighter cane and a thinner paddle. Instead, I chose ones that could do a good deal of damage. The holes in the paddle allow the paddle to swing through the air with less resistance, delivering a stronger blow.

"You should see how bright and red your ass is right now," I say. "I get the feeling, by the time we're done, we'll be adding the colors purple, black and blue. Do you know how many blows you're going to receive next if you don't answer correctly?"

When she doesn't answer, I take the cane from Vlad. "I asked you a question, pet."

"Eight," she replies, her voice breathy but not necessarily from fear.

"I was looking for the total number, which would be sixteen, so your answer is incorrect."

"You fu—" she starts to swear.

"Why don't you count for me, so I don't lose track of the number," I suggest before landing the first blow.

She cries out. One of her legs kicks up but is yanked back down by the shackles.

"Was that 'one' or should we start over?" I ask.

"One," she mumbles feebly.

I deliver another whack. She cries out louder. Even though Vlad is just as strong as me, he's not practiced in caning, so my strikes land more fully and accurately.

"Two," she says after a few pants.

She braces herself for the third one, which I land in the same place as the previous two to augment the pain.

"Fuck. Three," she spits out.

I allow the sting to sink in before delivering the fourth.

She gasps. "Four."

I decide to get evil on the fifth strike and cross it over the previous one.

"You keep answering my questions wrong and your ass is going to be shredded," I tell her before striking her three more times.

Her legs quiver. She seems to be sucking in her sobs.

"Where were we? Four?" I ask when she hasn't said anything.

"Seven! Seven!" she quickly blurts.

"Count faster next time," I advise. "This one will be number five."

I crack the cane against her bottom.

"Five."

The next two whacks ensure that she won't sit comfortably for days.

"Six...seven," she sniffles.

The final blow elicits her loudest scream yet. I hand the cane back to Vlad.

"Your turn," I say to Jack.

"Oh no," she murmurs as her knees buckle.

I go to get the chair and notice there are tears trickling down her cheeks and her nose has started to run. Taking the chair, I place it under her hips, using the back of the chair to prop her up.

Folding my arms, I stand in front of her. A whisper of guilt runs through me, but I force it down. In my world, there's no room for sympathy.

Jack wields the paddle like he's holding a baseball bat. The force could have knocked her halfway across the room if she wasn't locked into the pillory.

"Don't forget your count," I remind her, "or Jack will have to start all over."

"One!"

I can hear the desperation. Good.

"T-two," she stammers after Jack spanks her again.

Sniffling, she clenches her hands on the third blow. Her nails dig into her palms, but she remembers her count. On the next blow, her knuckles are white. By the seventh blow, she doesn't even try to stop her nose from running.

"Eight," she wails on the last spank.

I drink up the sight of her tears and snot, the sound of her ragged breaths and whimpers. That whisper of guilt flutters again. To prove I'm a heartless asshole to myself, I grab her cheeks and lick up one of her tears.

"Let's see how that ass is looking," I say as I step around to view her backside. A purple hue is starting to come in beneath the streaks of crimson.

"Gorgeous," I compliment as I place my hand over the curve of a buttock. Her skin is hot to the touch. "Why don't you give me the first name of your connect?"

"Please...there isn't anyone," she murmurs.

For a second, I almost believe her. Can she really be this strong, this resolved, this loyal?

"You realize that doubling the number means your ass is going to receive thirty-two strikes, sixteen from the cane and sixteen from the paddle?" I ask. "You think your ass is going to survive that?"

I grab a buttock and sink my fingers into the battered flesh, making her cry.

"How about just the first initial?" I try.

She draws in a shaky breath. "If I had some-one, I'd tell you, you fucking asshole!"

I can't help but admire her courage. She'd rather take a beating than give up the person or people she's working with. Who could they possibly be?

Releasing her, I run the back of my fingers lightly over the buttock. "They must be spe-cial to you for you to sacrifice your ass like this."

She moans. I pick up a different quality to this moan. Curious, I continue to brush the back of my hand lightly over her rump, tracing its contours. Her moan lengthens. In response, warmth stirs in my body.

"You haven't had your daily dose of omega blockers," I note. "Your body usually revert back to its natural state this quickly?"

"It's not," she says but not convincingly.

"What if I were to throw in a capsule of omega blocker and a bottle of cool, refreshing water to wash it down with?"

Silence. Is she considering my offer?

I let her think about it as I continue to caress her ass. It was a nice looking ass without the welts. With, it's even lovelier. And I'm an ass man. Even though Irene had a petite build, she had a full and beautiful rump.

"Please believe me. I'm here alone."

Her response surprises me. I'm offering her a damn good deal, and she'd still rather suffer through thirst and an ass beating?

I scent something, making the warmth in my groin swirl. Slipping my hand between her thighs, I connect with moisture. Not a lot but it's unmistakable. My blood pulses more strongly.

"Since my offer doesn't interest you, I've another game we can play," I tell her.

CHAPTER SEVENTEEN

VINCENT

S O FAR, FOUR GUYS on my security team have benefited from my pet. It's time I got a turn. I'm 99% positive that if I had her go down on me, she'd try to bite my dick off. But there are other delectable holes I can choose.

"This game is called 'Guess the Cock,'" I tell her as I replace my hand between her thighs and reach my middle finger toward her clitoris.

She tries to squirm from my touch, but it's not easy with the chair pressing up her hips.

"Make three correct guesses in a row, and you win a dish of water," I inform her.

On second thought, I should have designated a punishment for each wrong answer instead of rewarding correct answers, but I let it go.

Languidly, I brush my middle finger over her clit. She gasps. Her legs tremble. My cock throbs. The moisture between her legs increases.

"I take it you like the spanking, since you're up for more," I say. "Did you decide if you like the sting or the thudding pain more?"

She seems distracted by my fondling and doesn't answer. I pinch her clit and twist it.

"Neither," she squeals.

"Then we'll continue until you pick one."

For a good minute or so, I play with her clit, rolling it, petting it, twitching it. It swells beneath my touch. She's also wetter. Collecting some of her slick on my fingers, I walk to the other side of the pillory to show her. "You normally get this wet for men you hate?"

She looks livid. "That has nothing to do with you and everything to do with my rotten luck of being an omega. If I were a beta or an alpha, I'd rather fuck a warthog than you."

"That can be arranged," I inform her as I sniff at my fingers. She smells good. "Want to know how good you smell?"

I wipe her slick over her nostrils before going to the dresser, where I clean my fingers off with a towel. I grab a latex hood. She looks at it with misgiving as I approach her. I detach the nose hook from her. She must be relieved not to have her head forced back anymore.

"When I twist your nipple, you give me the name of the man fucking you," I explain. "If you guess correctly, I'll tap your shoulder once. Twice for an incorrect answer."

I pull the hood over her head and lace it up in back so that it fits tightly. There are no openings for the eyes and nose, only one for the mouth, and the area of the ears are padded, so she's deprived of sight, sound, and smell.

I nod at Jack and Vlad. They drop their pants and take out their cocks, which they stroke to full hardness. I point at Jack to go first. Taking his position, he rubs his tip along her folds a few times before sinking in. Watching him close his eyes and savor the wet heat embracing his cock makes mine stretch against my pants.

Reaching beneath her, I tug on her nipple.

"Jack," she returns.

I tap her shoulder and gesture to Vlad. "Next."

Reluctantly, Jack disengages from her and allows Vlad to take his spot. As I expected, Vlad goes in hard, slamming her into the pillory.

"Vlad!" she cries without prompting.

After giving her shoulder a tap, I instruct Jack to fuck her hard. He shoves into her just as hard, causing the chair to tip and making her come off her toes. I wave him off and twist her nipple.

After thinking for several seconds, she guesses, "Vlad."

I tap her shoulder twice, then tell Jack to go again. He changes his rhythm, going slower and more gently.

"Vlad," she guesses after I pinch her nipple.

Vlad takes over, inserting only his tip into her for several pumps.

"Jack," she guesses when prompted.

I tap her shoulder accordingly.

"You're just fucking with me," she says in frustration. "It doesn't matter if I'm guessing right or not!"

It's true. I could fuck with her in that way if I wanted to. But right now, she's messing up just fine on her own.

Vlad pulls out, then slams back into her. He pistons his hips roughly. Her tits swing from the force of it. Vlad grabs one of the orbs, manhandling it, squeezing it, slapping it.

"V-V-Vlad!" she exclaims when he twists her nipple.

"Now Jack," I instruct.

"Aw, man," Vlad grouses but obeys.

"She's so wet now," Jack says after sinking into her.

He buries himself to the hilt, then starts rolling his hips. She gives a shiver. The scent of sex has filled the room, but I detect her scent above it all. It's strong. And alluring. My cock pulses strongly.

"Ja...Jack," she sighs.

"You're gonna want to get some of this, boss," Jack says as he grabs her hips and thrusts into her deep.

"I plan to," I say, then jerk my head, gesturing for him to back off.

Standing behind her, I undo my pants, then stroke my cock as I admire her rump and the pussy lips below. Thanks to the beating, her ass is going to hurt for several days.

Reaching under her, I find there's a good amount of slick between her legs. Her scent travels through my nose, making the heat in my body churn. She whimpers when I caress her. Are the omega blockers out of her system already, or are her omega traits particularly potent? I continue to fondle her, drawing out more slick from her body, and inhale her thickening scent. Betas like Vlad and Jack detect only a whiff, but as an alpha, it's like her scent is made especially for me.

Upon hearing her soft moan, Vlad says, "I think she likes getting fucked by us."

I play with her engorged clit while Vlad and Jack look on. It's clear from their faces that they want back inside her. But she is all mine for now. My cock is close to fully hard, its knot already swollen. Lucky for her, the fucking she got from Vlad and Jack should have loosened her up. After coating my knob with her moisture, I start to press it into her slit. She swallows a whimper. I push harder as her pussy resists. Is she the type who likes to rip the bandage off fast or slow? I try the slow way first. She whines as my cock stretches her opening. I press and press. Her body tenses, which doesn't help her any. My knob doesn't pop in easily, so I opt for the fast way. Grabbing her hips with both hands, I thrust into her in one motion. She lets out a loud cry, one that reverberates off the walls.

Her wet heat washes over me. Why does she feel so good? My knot swells to its full size, locking me into her. For several beats, I remain motionless, soaking in the hot, wet embrace of her cunt, drinking up her erratic breathing as her body attempts to adjust to the intrusion.

She starts to grunt when I begin to roll my hips. She feels so amazing I want to come as soon as possible. At the same time, I want it to last long.

"Shit!" she cries when I push myself deeper.

Vlad smiles. I know he wants me to take her pussy to task. I decide to oblige and slam into her hard. The pillory shakes and creaks. The lock rattles with my thrusting. The place fills with the sound of her cries and my pelvis slapping into her ass.

"Fuck me," Vlad swears in Russian.

I slow to give her a break and the chance to win her dish of water. I give her nipple a vicious twist.

"Vincent," she returns without a shred of doubt in her voice.

I'm pleased she knows it's me. I give her shoulder a tap and a brief moment for her to rejoice in her win before I go back to ravaging her pussy. Her gasping cries resume, though not as stridently as before.

There's no going back now. If I try to pull out of her before I come, I'll rip her pussy. Her body has accepted my invading cock and wets it with more and more slick. My head swims with how glorious it feels to slide my flesh against hers. Groans now intermix with her grunts as I fall into a steadier rhythm to draw out the pleasure. I catch her pussy fluttering against me. I detect a different quality in her groans–desire instead of despair. I think she might climax. I angle my cock to improve its chances of grazing against her clit.

"No..." she whispers.

I wouldn't want to come for my rapist either. But her body wants it.

"Undo her hood and set the mirror in front of her," I instruct Jack.

With her hood off, I can plainly see the dismay on her face reflected in the mirror.

"You're going to come for me, pet," I tell her.

"No fucking way," she spits, but I think she's trying to convince herself more than she is me.

"You want to bet on that, pet?"

Her silence betrays her lack of confidence.

"Bet you didn't know you were such a slut," I say, knowing full well it has nothing to do with her being a slut or not.

"I'm an omega. You've figured that out."

"And that makes you a slut by nature. It's in your DNA."

CHAPTER EIGHTEEN

VINCENT

"AND THAT MAKES YOU a slut by nature. It's in your DNA."

I can tell my words burn into her because she has to acknowledge it's true at some level. It's not her fault she was born this way. Some people accept and even fully embrace being an omega. I can tell she's not one of them. She'll probably never admit it, but my omega blockers are a source of freedom for people like her. They liberate her to be in command of their own bodies, to shake off the shackles of their genetics.

I roll my hips tenderly, finding the rhythm and depth that makes her legs quiver. Her brow furrows with worry as she fights her own arousal. I remove the chair from under her so that I can better reach around her hip to stroke her clit.

She tries to jerk from my touch, but I hold her firmly with my other hand.

"No, no," she gasps.

Closing her eyes, she grimaces. I wonder what awful things she has to imagine to cool her ardor. I get the feeling she'd rather eat shit than come for me.

"I like the way your pussy flexes against my cock," I say wickedly.

"I'm trying to get you to come, you asshole," she lies.

"Nice try, but you're going to come first because that's what sluts do."

She goes silent, but no matter how hard she concentrates, her body is losing the battle. Her pussy caresses my cock as I fondle her clit and bury myself with deep languid thrusts. Occasionally a grunt escapes her lips. Through it all, I can sense her desire intensifying and am not at all surprised when her body starts to convulse and she blurts out a cry, followed by a groan with one part misery and ten parts pleasure. The heat and moisture in her pussy increases. Her orgasm feels amazing on my cock. Fucking amazing.

"Good sluts always come for their master," I say to rub it in.

After a few more tremors go through her body, I grab her hips and work on my own release. Switching up the pace, I go for fast and furious, pounding into her so hard her teeth chatter. She can't even cry out properly. My knot expands right before my climax, which is intense, as if I've had blue balls for months. My body tenses as I spill my load into her pulsing warmth. Rapture throbs deep in my bones, and it takes me a while to recover.

My body reels from the experience, like that of someone who's been wandering the desert and is overwhelmed by the jugs of water he drinks to quench his thirst. A strong shudder goes through me, making me grunt. As unsuccessfully as she tried to hold off from orgasming, I realize I couldn't have held back either. Not when her pussy was so incredibly sweet. Usually I don't have issues holding back from climaxing.

After the swelling of my knot recedes enough to pull out of her, I let Vlad and Jack finish. My head still swims, and my body buzzes with rapture. While in the afterglow, I watch as Vlad pounds into her. As he comes, he pulls out and sprays his cum over her ass and lower back.

"Really?" Jack complains to Vlad. "Now your shit's going to get on me."

Vlad returns a large grin.

"Mother fucker," Jack grumbles before sinking himself into her.

He has to hold her up because her legs look ready to buckle. He takes his time thrusting into her until the end, when he accelerates his pummeling to send himself over the edge.

She looks ready to collapse, though doing so won't feel good while her neck and wrists are still locked in the pillory. I tell my men to take her out.

"And get her a dish of water," I instruct.

They set her on her knees, and Vlad pinions her arms behind her while Jack places a dish of water before her.

"Go on, drink your fill," I tell her.

With Vlad still holding her, she leans forward and slurps up the water. She licks the dish clean.

"Put her back in the cage," I say when she finishes.

I'm perturbed at myself for not enjoying the fact that she has to drink her water as if she were actually a four-legged pet of mine. In fact, I feel off altogether.

Done with her for the day, I return to my suite. I could join the rest of my guests for dinner, but I've never been much of a social person, and I have a low tolerance for people who talk too much. Charlie sometimes gets that way. People say he has charisma, and maybe that would be an interesting change for the Black Dragon Triad. I'm an introvert, and I don't plan on changing.

Letting the salty air blow at me out on the balcony, I pour *baiju* into a porcelain cup and down it.

"Come in," I respond to Esen announcing himself.

"Still nothing on Irene Lazzarelli," he informs. "And I'm looking into the circle of family and friends of people we've killed or pissed off. No Irene Lazzarelli there either. It's like she's off the grid."

"She gave me a fake name," I say, throwing back another cup of *baiju*. Goddammit. Why do I feel so unsettled?

"You think so?"

Recalling the way hate blazed in her eyes when she looked at me, I reply, "Yes. To hide people she cares about. Or to fuck with me."

"She'll give in eventually."

I think about what she's been through so far, but she doesn't seem any closer to giving me the answers. I'm going to have to up the game.

And for some strange fucking reason, I'm having second thoughts about that. All I know I definitely want to do is to fuck her again.

"'Eventually' could mean weeks," I say. "I had planned to kill her in the next day or two."

"Have you tried waterboarding?"

"I haven't. I should."

As the words come out of my mouth, I feel an odd sensation. What would Irene think of me now? She'd loathe the monster I've become. There were times I thought maybe she was aware of my darker side, which I had hid from her to the best of my ability, and loved me anyway. But she could never love me if she knew what I had done since her passing. In my pain and desperation to find her killers, I had been reckless at first. I had beaten up people who, it turned out later, were innocent.

If Fate had given me just a few more months, my life would have been completely different. Even though there had been talk for over a year that I might be selected to become the next head dragon, I had planned to quit the triad completely and live the rest of my days with

Irene. I would have been a father. I didn't have one of my own growing up, so I was nervous. But I was excited. It didn't matter if it was going to be a girl or a boy, I was going to try my best.

Instead, after Irene's death, I threw myself into the triad more than ever. After initially failing to find the people who took away the most perfect person in the world, I decided I needed to be in a position of power if I wanted to scorch the earth in my search for vengeance. I did find the men who shot her, and I tortured them for months. One of the two committed suicide. The other unexpectedly choked to death. The name of the person they said ordered the hit turned out to be fake. That's who I want to squeeze the life out of with my bare hands. Until that happens, I have unfinished business.

"You okay, boss?" Esen asks when I pour a third cup of *baiju*. "You might as well drink razor blades."

"Yeah," I agree as the liquid burns my throat. I don't consume a lot of alcohol, but for some reason this attempted assassination has brought up the ghosts of my past, ghosts that I want to wash away.

Dammit.

That fucking little bitch. The least she could have done is succeed in her attempt to kill me. When I find out who she really is, I'll kill her and her whole family.

Suddenly I see Irene's face. She's horrified at my intentions.

Mother fucker.

"What are the guests up to?" I ask Esen.

"Charlie's in the hot tub with Rusakov and some women."

I rub my temples.

"Why don't you join them, boss?" Esen suggests. "Relax and enjoy yourself. Get a brand of *baiju* that won't rip your insides."

Even though I don't feel particularly social, I decide to take Esen up on his idea. Putting on swim trunks, I head to the pool and hot tub area. As Esen described, Charlie, Rusakov, and four women sit in the hot tub. Two of the women hold champagne glasses. Charlie has a cigar dangling from his mouth. Upon seeing me, he puts out his cigar because I'm not much of smoker.

"Shit. Didn't know you were going to join us, Vince," he says.

One of the two blondes brightens when she sees me. "Now we have a better ratio of guys to girls. Champagne?"

"Vince is more of a tea drinker," Charlie tells her.

The brunette, Katiya, detaches herself from Rusakov and sits next to me. "I like tea."

Jimena, a buxom beauty whom I suspect likes the women Charlie hangs out with more than Charlie himself, stands and situates herself on my other side. Charlie frowns at her movement. He's had the hots for Jimena for years. She strings him along to pay for her luxury apartment, her car, and her shopping.

"*El dragón* finally emerges from his den," Jimena purrs. "I don't think I've ever seen you in a hot tub before."

"What's the occasion?" Charlie asks.

"What do you mean?" I return as Jimena places her hand on my thigh beneath the bubbling water. I notice her floss swimwear barely covers her inflated tits.

"Not that I'm complaining, but you don't usually socialize."

"Feeling restless, I guess."

"We can help, yes?" Katiya offers.

I think back to how amazing it felt to have my cock buried in "Ramona." That's what I want more of. Could I possibly be in a rut? I don't think my little caged omega is in heat. She's only been off her omega blockers for a day. Maybe I just need pussy. It has nothing to do with my assassin.

"Katiya—she is very good at taking away the restlessness," Rusakov vouches with a sly grin.

Smiling up at me, Katiya places her hand on my crotch. My cock stirs.

I accept and, hopping out, sit on the edge of the hot tub. Katiya positions herself between my legs and pulls down the waistband of my swim trunks.

The taller of the two blondes straddles Rusakov. "Now I have you all to myself."

As Katiya pulls out my cock and envelops it in her mouth, the blonde and Rusakov start to kiss. Charlie motions for Jimena, but she chooses to stay where she is.

Katiya goes to work on my cock. I wonder if Ramona is any good at giving head. It doesn't matter. It'll feel great when I ravish her mouth against her will.

"Let me have a taste," Jimena says to Katiya.

Replacing Katiya, Jimena wraps her thick lips, filled with whatever is the latest shit, around my shaft. Irene had naturally plump lips. And a shapely ass.

Jimena sucks harder than Katiya, and I reward her by shoving my cock deeper into her throat. Charlie watches while his blonde attaches her mouth to his neck.

"My turn," Katiya says, poking Jimena when she doesn't come off.

After letting Katiya take over, Jimena starts playing with her tits. Tension roils in my groin.

"You want to fuck these, you can," invites Jimena, pulling out an orb and sticking out her long tongue to lick her own nipple.

"Hot damn," Charlie mutters.

I let Katiya blow me until I come, but I hold back the ejaculation.

"Why no cum?" Katiya asks.

"Because I'm saving it for Tits," I reply.

Picking up Katiya, I sit her near the edge of the tub and spread her legs open. I pull the ties at the sides of her bikini bottom. The garment falls off to reveal her mound. Getting back in the water, I grab Jimena by the hair and shove her into Katiya's snatch. While Jimena goes down on Katiya, I stand behind Jimena, pull aside her bathing suit, and jam my cock into her. She cries out into Katiya's crotch. Grabbing her hips, I ram myself against her ass, which has also been cosmetically augmented.

"Eat her out good," I order, slowing down so she can focus on the cunnilingus.

Katiya moans. "Yes. So good."

Charlie drinks in the sight. Rusakov grunts in Russian as he comes.

After Katiya releases a soft cry in her climax, I resume my pounding of Jimena's cunt. She braces herself against the edge of the tub so she doesn't get her face slammed into the side and lose her teeth. The water sloshes about with our movement, splashing up into her face.

"*Dios mio! Dios mio!*" she cries as my knot swells inside of her.

As I slam into her, I imagine myself thrusting into Ramona. I remember how wet and hot and tight her pussy had felt. It felt the best when she came.

With a roar, I release the pressure in my groin, filling Jimena with cum even though I came not too long ago. Her legs buckle after I withdraw from her.

"*Dios mio,*" she sighs.

I can tell Charlie wants Jimena bad, but he probably doesn't want to go after me.

"Shit, that was hard fucking you give to her," Rusakov says.

"Actually, I was holding back," I tell him. *Because I'm saving some for Ramona.*

"I think poor Jimena could use some love," Charlie tells his blonde, who goes over to Jimena.

The two women start kissing.

I sit down and lean my head back against the edge, looking up at the stars in the night sky while the hot water rumbles over my body.

Rusakov gestures for one of the servers and tells her to bring him vodka.

"You want also?" he asks me.

I shake my head and close my eyes. I can't fucking believe this. I just got sucked off by Katiya, shot my load into Jimena, and my body still doesn't feel satiated. It still craves *her*.

I get out of the hot tub and return to my room to shower off. I could try to go to sleep, but it would be fruitless. What I need is another visit to the dungeon.

CHAPTER NINETEEN

MARTINA

BECAUSE MY BODY PRODUCED so much slick, I feel more dehydrated than ever. I can't remember ever feeling this battered or this dirty. I'm sticky with my own piss, tears, slick, and cum. All of that, however, pales to the disgust I feel at having come for Vincent and that his cum burns inside of me. It takes its time seeping out of me though I try to push it out. I had hoped that my hatred for Vincent could overpower my body's primal urges, and even though I know it's not my fault, I can't help but be disappointed.

I'm not a slut.

Vincent said what he did to get under my skin, and even if he does regard me as a slut, why should I care what the hell he thinks? I wish there was a way to get under his skin. Probably not the smartest thing to irritate the guy when he gets to call the shots, but at least I can go down swinging.

But I know so little about Vincent outside his ruthless reputation and his leadership as the head of the Black Dragon Triad. I tried digging into everything about him. Raised the son of a single mother, he doesn't seem to have any family left. He was never married. Doesn't seem to have a partner. No kids. His mother died when he was a teen. His uncle seemed to be how he got involved in the triad to begin with, but that uncle committed suicide several years ago.

What could possibly be his Achilles' heel?

As I consider how I might hit him where it hurts, I try to find a comfortable position in the cage. I would rather lay on my back than on my side, but my ass is too tender. I want to sleep, but there's still some arousal left in my body. I keep reliving the fucking I got. It hurt. My shoulders are bruised from being slammed into the pillory. Every time their pelvis smacked into my backside, they reawakened the sting from the cane and the ache from the paddle.

At first their penetration produced nothing but pain, their cocks bruising me from the inside. Initially, I thought my body produced slick to protect itself, but there was no denying the flutter of pleasure in my clit when Vincent caressed me. It had felt so good even though my mind screamed in protest. Everything Vincent did thereafter felt good, except when he pushed his swollen knot into me right before climaxing. My pussy had never felt so stretched. I hate the fact that his sperm is swimming inside of me. To be impregnated by my mortal enemy would be a fate worse than death, so it's a good thing he's going to kill me soon.

A week ago I wouldn't be surprised to be dead at this time. The night before we boarded Vincent's yacht, Brady and I had had sex. We were both feeling fatalistic, figuring we might as well do something nice for ourselves in what could be our final days alive. It wasn't our first time having sex, and there wasn't any romance to it. While Brady is a good-looking guy and a good lover in bed, I haven't been in the mindset for a relationship since the massacre of my family.

The sex between Brady and me would qualify as romantic compared to what I just went through, where I was used and abused, my body serving their purposes, an unwilling participant for their pleasure. And even though I'm painfully aware of that, a part of me wants it again. Desire swirls in my lower belly when I close my eyes and recall the shivers of pleasure that went through me when Vincent slid in and out of me. The wetness between my legs grows. I stroke myself there and bring the moisture to my clit. How does Vincent know to elicit such strong reactions from me? Does he have that effect on all omegas, or is my body particularly thirsty for his touch?

I don't want to be thinking of Vincent while I masturbate, so I force myself to think about Brady instead and how good it felt when he went down on me. His cunnilingus was top-notch. I came for him twice our last night together.

But Vincent invades my thoughts. My favorite position is doggy style, and his angle of penetration when I was locked in the pillory was superb. When he added touching my clitoris, it was all over.

I quicken my fondling, glad that my hands are free.

"Well, we are quite slutty, aren't we?"

I bolt into a sitting position, hitting my head on the top of the cage while pain angrily flares in my ass.

How did Vincent manage to enter so quietly? And how is he able to see so well in the dark?

"What's the matter? You didn't get fucked enough earlier?" he asks after approaching my cage.

Is he alone? I wonder hopefully.

As if in answer to my question, I hear Jack clear his throat.

"Don't let us interrupt you," Vincent says. "Let's see how you play with that pretty pussy of yours."

I don't move a muscle.

"I've got a nice bottle of water waiting for you if you put on a good show for us."

"Let me see," I say.

He sets down a glass bottle next to the cage. It looks like fifty milliliter's worth of delicious water. Will he let me drink the whole thing? That bottle of water is worth more than gold to me. And more than my pride.

Reluctantly I lean back against the side of the cage and spread my legs. He shines his cell phone light on me, casting everything behind it in darkness, making me more aware of my exposure. I slide my fingers along my clit.

"Next time I fuck her harder for you, boss," Vlad offers.

"Would you like that, pet?" Vincent asks me.

Vincent sits alone on the top of my enemies list. Second is the man who shot my family, but Vlad is coming in a close third at the moment.

As more slick flows out of me, Vincent inhales deeply. He gives his phone to Vlad to hold and walks behind me. Even though my body is on alert for what he might do, I don't stop playing with myself. I want to and I don't want to come in front of these guys.

Grabbing the leash, Vincent yanks me against the cage with one hand while he reaches through the cage with his other and grabs one of my breasts. The rash has faded significantly, unlike the welts on my rump. For a second I consider digging my nails into his arm, but what good would that do? Plus, I really want that bottle of water. He mauls my orb, digging his fingers into it, kneading it, slapping it. He tugs and rolls the nipple, which feels like it will be forever tender. The arousal between my legs takes away from some of the pain.

His hand joins mine, and instantly pleasure and desire swell.

"I can do this on my own," I hiss.

"I know you can. I'm just showing you how every inch of your body is mine to play with.

Your nipples. Your ass. Your pussy. Even your orgasms are mine."

"Under duress," I qualify. "If I wasn't an omega, I'd never orgasm for you."

What I said seems to give him pause. I can't have possibly wounded his pride?

"You sure about that?" he returns.

"Hell yes."

"We could take away your omega qualities with the blockers. Would you like that?"

That's a dilemma. Originally, I had wanted them without question because I didn't want to be here: wet with desire at his touch. But what are the benefits of taking the omega blockers? Whether I do or don't doesn't alter my mental state. I hate Vincent. I want him dead. And I would give anything not to have his hands on me. At least without the blockers, my body won't be in so much pain, though it might be worth it if Vincent prefers it that way. I wouldn't take the blockers just to spite him.

"What do you think?" he asks as he resumes gently stroking my clit. "What do you prefer?"

I prefer you to get your fucking hands off of me.

No you don't, counters my body, which is melting beneath his skilled fingers.

What would he prefer? Would he rather see me screaming in pain if I take blockers? Or does he prefer to see me screaming in pleasure if I go without the blockers?

"It sucks for you either way, doesn't it?" he asks rhetorically. "Because the omega blockers only affect the physical qualities of being an omega. Your mind, your emotions stay the same. The blockers don't change the fact that you hate me touching you like this. I win either way, don't I, pet?"

His fingers circle my slit, teasing me. I swallow a whimper, finding myself wishing he would press his digits into me.

But he heard me. "What was that, pet?"

Fuck you, asshole. Please fuck me.

I don't answer aloud while the conflict rages inside of me.

"Did you want me inside you?" he asks.

Vlad answers for me. "Course she does, boss. I've never seen a slut get so wet before."

"Shut up." Vince sounds slightly annoyed. To me, he says in a tone that's half menacing, half seductive, "Answer me, pet."

It doesn't matter what I respond, Vincent will do whatever he wants to do, and I can't stop him. Nevertheless, I don't want to verbalize such a desire.

He sinks his finger into my wet heat. My pussy clutches at him hungrily.

"I think I have my answer," he pronounces.

I glare inwardly at my own body. *Traitor.*

He sinks a second finger into me while I continue to caress my clit. God, this feels so good. More slick flows out of me, pooling beneath my ass.

"Vlad is right," Vincent says. "You are one slutty omega. I've been with many in my lifetime, and none of them got as wet as you."

"That doesn't mean shit," I tell him. "There is no correlation."

"You can tell yourself that, but you know the truth."

Angry, I try to move away from his touch, but he yanks on my leash harder. His fingers slide in deeper. They brush against a more sensitive spot inside me. I still immediately, wanting him to graze that area again.

"Let's try a different metric: the intensity and frequency of your orgasms," he suggests.

I don't contest him on that. An orgasm sounds really good right about it now. I think I might even want it more than I want the bottle of water. The more Vincent strokes me inside, the more I want to come. His curled fingers strike that sensitive spot over and over. Sinking into the pleasure fluttering through my pussy, I don't need to caress my clit.

But Vincent says, "Keep playing with yourself. Because that's what sluts do."

I hate this. There is the illusion of choice because he's not forcibly taking my hand and making me do it, so it seems like I'm acquiescing to his statement about being a slut.

Vlad nudges Jack. "Look how big her clit gets. Such a whore."

Cheeks flushing, I imagine taking an ax to Vlad's head.

But desire calls to me. I tune out Vlad and resume touching myself. Combined with Vincent's fingers curled deliciously inside me, my masturbation quickly sends me toward the edge. I gasp when he intensifies his stroking.

"You like that, do you?" Vincent asks when my gasps turn into whimpers and pants. "Does the slut want to come?"

I shouldn't care what the hell Vincent calls me, but I hate that he's getting away with it, that there's nothing I can do to stop him from using that sexist, pejorative term.

He slows his fondling. "I asked you a question, slut."

Even though he knows I damn well want to come, I stubbornly don't want to admit it.

When I stay silent, he withdraws his fingers.

Noooo.

I try to make up for his absence by fondling myself faster, but he grabs both my wrists and pulls them through the cage.

"Sluts like you don't get to come without permission," he informs me, "and to get permission, you need to answer my question."

Fuck you. The answer is fuck you.

But the deep, wet craving pulses between my legs. I want to cross the finish line. He lets me stew in my silence while unbuckling and whipping off his belt. He uses it to tie my wrists behind me, outside the cage.

"Does this mean you don't want to come?"

If I answer yes, am I admitting to being a slut? I squirm with conflict and desire. He reaches through the cage for my clit. His touch sends a current through me. He keeps his strokes light and languid, teasing me with potential while drawing me closer to that beautiful climax my body sorely needs, that I deserve after all I've been through.

"Well, pet?"

I hate that his fingers feel even better than my own. I relent. "Yes."

"You sure about that?"

Of course I'm sure, you fucker.

"Then beg. Beg to come."

Beg?!

No fucking way.

CHAPTER TWENTY

VINCENT

I DON'T NEED TO see her expression to know that begging to come is probably the last thing she would want to do. She hasn't even begged me for her life and would probably prefer to stick a rusty nail through her eye than ask me for anything. But I smell her potent desire. I feel her body quivering with need. She can't resist her carnal calling. She can try, but she won't succeed. I don't rush her. Her feeble attempt to suppress her primal urges amuse me. The only problem is my own growing lust. Normally I'm a patient man, but her snatch felt so damn good about my fingers. My body is alert to her every move, and even the unevenness of her breath arouses me.

"Beg to come," I reiterate while I continue to fondle her swollen bud. "Beg for me, slut."

"Fuck you."

So she wants to play the spitfire. That's fine. I know how to deal with brats. I sink my fingers back into her cunt and find her G-spot. She immediately starts to pant.

"You think by not begging, you're not a slut? Don't kid yourself. You want to come. I can prove it. I can rip one out of you right now. Only a slut, after being whipped with nettle, her ass beaten black and blue, her body dirty with her own piss and the cum of three different guys, can still find it in herself to come."

I make sure my hand hits both her clit and her G-spot while my other hand gropes her breast. She grunts when I pull on the nipple, the pain balancing the pleasure below. I pinch the nipple hard. Her body strains in my hands, both seeking and avoiding me. Her cunt presses against my fingers. Part of me wants to make her come, to feel her spasming against me. But I'm not that nice.

I fondle her more, working up the agitation in her body before withdrawing, leaving her bereft. I hear a soft whine escape her lips before she breathes in through clenched teeth. Her body trembles.

"You sure you don't want to beg?"

She draws a long breath, herself. I disrupt her effort by brushing her clit. She bites her lower lip and closes her eyes. I wonder if she's trying to transport herself somewhere else. I pinch and twist her nipple to bring her back. I give her cunt another taste of my fingers. Her snatch clamps down my digits.

"Beg. You know you want it," I urge her as I piston my fingers in and out of her. Her wet cunt makes slurping, squishing sounds. "Hear that? I've never heard such a loud pussy before. Does your daddy know you're such a slut?"

I know there's no correlation between arousal and wetness. I know the vagina can lubricate itself even when penetrated against a woman's will. But I wanted to fuck with her, as I did earlier. And it worked. She was pissed.

"Does your mother know you're such an asshole?" she retorts.

I give a rueful chuckle.

The truth is my mother would be beyond disappointed, sickened, devastated, but I've already apologized to her. Spiritually. If there's such a thing as a next life, I'll spend it making it up to her. And Irene.

"Then we make an interesting pair," I say. "An asshole and a slut."

Her only comeback is a snort. She's more interested in arching her pussy against my hand.

Wickedly, I stop my fondling and carefully remove my fingers. My groin throbs with desire, but I'm not done toying with her. "Answer my question, slut."

She seems preoccupied, so I slap her cheek to focus her.

"What question?" she huffs.

"Does your daddy know you're such a slut?" I repeat.

As if she can see me, she glares ahead of herself.

I brush my fingers over her folds. "It's not a rhetorical question, pet. Does he know? Your hesitation makes me think the answer is 'yes.' Maybe he more than knows. Maybe he's sampled your slutty cunt for himself."

"You're a sick fucker."

Grabbing her by her jaw, I turn her so her ear is near my mouth. "So you've said. But you don't know the half of it, pet. And I'm happy to show you all my sick fuckery."

I lick the side of her face. "So how was daddy? Did you come for him? You ride his cock like a good little slut?"

She looks disgusted.

"Did he take care of you well and made sure you got to come everyday? Was he a good daddy?"

She tries to wrest her jaw free from my grip, to get away from the dirty, taboo visions my words generate.

"He was obviously better than yours," she spits. "You inherit your sick fuckery from him? Or did that come from your mother's side? Wait. It's got to be both because you've got it in spades."

"Bringing my mother into this? That's a low blow. Believe it or not, my mother was a good person. But I'll be the first to admit my dad was a worthless fuck. So, yeah, I've got his genes. But the interesting thing about your dad is that the thought of fucking him has made you more wet."

"Bullshit."

Still holding her by the jaw, I reach between her legs with my other hand and scoop her cunt juices onto my middle and forefinger. I hold it up to her. "See that, slut? I wonder, if we keep talking about your daddy, can you come without me even having to touch you?"

"Go fuck yourself."

I chuckle. "Why do that when I can fuck *you*?"

She turns color.

I bring my fingers to her lips. "Go on. Taste yourself."

She doesn't budge.

I threaten, "You want me to make this hurt?"

When she parts her lips, I slip my fingers into her mouth and wipe her slick onto her tongue. "Now suck my fingers clean."

She wraps her lips around my digits. The pressure, the warmth, and the wetness of her mouth makes my body throb with desire. I start to finger fuck her the way I'd like to shove my cock into her. She gags when my fingers press down on the back of her tongue. Without giving her a chance to collect herself, I stuff all four of my fingers into her mouth, stretching her mouth wide. Hearing her gag and feeling her struggle gets my ardor pumping even more.

I continue to mess with her. "Do you miss your daddy? Miss his cock? How would he feel if he could see his little girl now? Do you think he'd be sad...or turned on?"

I withdraw my fingers from her mouth so she can stop gagging and to give her a chance to answer.

"Which is it?" I press.

"He'd want to blow your head off – after he cut off your balls and shoved them down your throat."

Not bad for an answer. I smirk. "So he'd be jealous of me. But if he was a good daddy who cared about his little girl, he'd want to make sure his baby was taken care of."

I return to fondling her clit. She closes her eyes, but after a few minutes, the quality of her breath changes. Shorter, more shallow. Her juices continue to flow as I stroke her. Patiently, I fondle her till she tenses with the need to come.

"Don't forget to beg," I murmur near her ear.

She grunts. She won't do it, so I withdraw my hand. She whimpers.

"What's that? You want to come?" I ask and briefly caress her clit.

She shudders and whispers, "Yes."

"I'll let you come, baby girl. You just have to beg for it."

I toy with her pleasure bud, teasing her toward the edge but always stopping short.

Her pride wrestles with her desire. The latter wins.

"Please."

"Please what?" I ask.

"Please can I come?" she mumbles.

"I didn't hear that."

She asks louder, "Please, can I come?"

"Is that the best you can do?"

She groans. "Please, please make me come."

"Begging your enemy. You must want it bad. That right?"

"Yes."

"Yes, what?"

"Yes, I want to come bad."

"Only sluts want to come this bad. Are you a slut, baby girl?"

Her body strains, stretching, reaching for that delicious climax. But I slow my fondling again. The scent of her desire fills up the whole space, invading my senses. I can't remember when I felt a greater need to fuck something. But I want to continue tormenting her.

"Yes," she submits.

Still an asshole, I ask, "Yes what?"

"Yes, I'm a slut."

"Say it louder."

"I'm a slut!"

"Louder."

"I'm. A. Slut."

My ears drink up her words.

"You catch all that?" I ask Vlad.

"I've been video recording it all, boss."

"Make sure you get this slut coming."

"You got it, boss."

Turning back to her, I say, "Tell you what. Since your daddy isn't here to take care of his little girl, I'll do it for him. Get on your hands and knees for daddy."

After untying her wrists, I reach between the bars, grab her ankles and pull her legs out of the cage She doesn't object. I shift onto my knees and pull down my pants. My hardened cock springs to attention, eager to taste that slopping wet pussy. Grabbing her hips, I pull her towards me until her ass, still red from its earlier beating, presses against the bars of the cage. She cries out when the bars dig into her raw backside.

I slide my length along her slit before rubbing my tip into her clit. "How badly do you want your daddy to fuck his baby girl?"

She only moans.

"You can tell us. We know you're a slut who gives it up for her daddy. And you miss him, don't you?"

She gives an anguished cry. I think I hit a nerve. I try hitting it again. "Sounds like you miss your daddy a lot. He must've taken care of his little girl often. Since he's not here, you want me to be your daddy?"

I withdraw my cock. Her pussy clenches at nothing.

"Yes," she murmurs.

Satisfied, I shove my hips and impale her on my cock. She feels incredible, as delicious as ever, even after the three of us have loosened her up.

Gradually I start to rock my hips. "Is this how your daddy fucked you?"

"He didn't!"

I stop my thrusting. "How did he fuck you, then? In the ass? Did he pop both your cherries?"

"Ugh."

I smile at what an asshole I can be. "Then tell me. How did your daddy like to fuck you? Did he fuck you hard like this?"

I pound into her ferociously. She cries out from the force of it.

"I'm sorry. Was your daddy more gentle?"

"Yes!"

"Too bad I'm not him."

Though the cage bars are in the way, I fuck her so hard her hands slip from under her. She tries to crawl from me but I grab her hips. I want to ravage her pussy till there's nothing left but decide to give her a reprieve after several minutes of hard pounding.

Dropping one of my hands, I play with her clit. "I want to hear how a good little girl begs for daddy to fuck her."

She groans. "Just fuck me already, please."

"Say 'please, daddy, please fuck me.'"

"Please, daddy, please fuck me."

"Now tell me why."

When she doesn't respond, I take my hand away.

"Because your baby girl needs it bad," she says.

"That's more like it. Tell me more."

"Your baby girl loves it when you fuck me with your big daddy cock."

The blood pounds in my ears. I roll my hips and feel the flutter of her pussy over my cock. "That feel good, baby girl?"

"Yes, daddy. Fuck me more, daddy."

"Keep going."

"You fuck your little girl so good, daddy. You're gonna make me come so hard, daddy."

Hearing that, it takes all of me not to drill the hell out of her.

"Who's daddy's good little cum slut?" I ask.

"I am."

"You gonna come hard for me, baby girl?"

"Yes, daddy! Yes, I—"

Her last words end in a wail. While I buck into her, I agitate my fingers without pause over her swollen clit. She emits another cry, her body quaking, arching, flushing. Breathing in her climax, I relish every tremor, every soft moan, until her convulsions send me over the edge. I drive myself relentlessly into her before my knot swells, locking me to her cunt. Tension coils deep inside me and releases with a fury. My body bucks hard, bruising my pelvis against the cage. I vaguely hear her gasping cries as my cum pours into her, mixing with her wet heat. When I finally disengage from her, my head still spins. The thudding of my heartbeat remains loud and fast.

Holy fuck. I did not think I could come like that, having come less than an hour before. Despite feeling spent, a part of me wants to go at her again.

She lays collapsed in the cage, her eyes closed, her chest heaving, her cheeks flushed. The afterglow of orgasm looks stunning on her.

"I got daddy's little slut all on camera," Vlad tells me.

After pulling up my pants, I sit down on the floor and collect myself. I've never been affected by an omega like this before. Even though I came, I don't feel like I've had my fill of her. All the more reason to kill her sooner rather than later.

Or...

I get up and retrieve my phone from Vlad.

"Give her the bottle of water," I instruct him, "and have the kitchen send down some bread or something."

I hadn't planned on feeding her. No sense in nourishing someone who isn't going to last the week. But I've changed my mind.

I'm going to let her live. I'm going to keep her as my pet. There's a lot of sick and twisted shit I could do to her. And I want to do them all.

Only it's not just her body that belongs to me. I want her fucking soul to possess.

Made in United States
Orlando, FL
25 June 2024

48293936R00091